# A GOLD SATIN MURDER

A Casey Holland Mystery Novella

Debra Purdy Kong

Gypsy Moon Press
British Columbia, Canada
2022

# A GOLD SATIN MURDER

(Casey Holland Mysteries #7)

www.debrapurdykong.com
ISBN: 978-1-9991987-5-6

Editor: Joyce Gram
www.gramediting.com

Jacket Design: Jim Bisakowski
http://bookdesign.ca

# AUTHOR'S NOTES

This seventh Casey Holland mystery picks up Casey's story just over a year after events in book #6, *The Blade Man*. *A Gold Satin Murder* takes place in the summer of 2015, long before the Covid pandemic. Therefore, you won't find any reference to mask-wearing which, as I write this, is still common among local transit users.

Many thanks to a great group of writers from Port Moody's Creative Writing workshops who provided terrific feedback during the first draft. Also, a huge thank you to beta readers Darlene Foster, Deborah White, Jo-Anne McLean, and Tamara Gorin for their invaluable comments. A huge shout-out goes to my editor Joyce Gram who knows so much more about grammar than I ever will.

Last but not least, hugs and gratitude to my husband and family, who fulfill me in so many ways and give me the space and time to live a creative life.

# ONE

After a decade of security work for Mainland Public Transport, Casey Holland had learned that troublesome passengers were usually rude, loud, and poorly dressed. But the gorgeous, broad-shouldered man in the charcoal suit, white shirt, and bright red tie strutting down the aisle was a new, intriguing challenge.

The moment the man spotted Casey, he gave her a broad, toothy smile. Cool. Her silky, low-cut tank top and dangling crystal earrings were doing their job. Undercover assignments rarely involved dressing up, but passenger complaints about a hot guy who'd been badgering women to model for his paintings required a different fashion choice. Besides, the bus was way too warm this late-July evening. The less she had to wear the better.

Casey winked at the man, then tilted her head toward the empty seat next to her. He slowed his pace and nodded to the gaping middle-aged woman he passed by. Judging from a quick survey, the man had caught the attention of most passengers. The men didn't look as impressed as the women, though.

"Hola, señorita." Gold-flecked brown eyes glanced at her hands as he sat down. "I am Eduardo from Ecuador."

"Casey. From Vancouver," she replied. "How are ya?" To reveal she was a señora who'd been happily married for just over a year might put him off, so the wedding rings stayed home.

"Excelente." He beamed. "I am here only three months, but I am in love with Vancouver. It has many interesting people."

"That it does." His cedarwood and vanilla cologne sent a jolt of nostalgia through Casey. When Dad was alive, she occasionally gave him a bottle of something similarly scented for Father's Day. She sat up straighter and zeroed in on Eduardo. Not the time for reflection.

"I apologize if my English is not so good," Eduardo said.

"It sounds fine to me." She smiled. "Do you live in this part of the city?"

"Si. Only one block away. I love to walk and ride the buses and talk to people."

He'd have many opportunities to do exactly that in Vancouver's densely populated West End. Thanks to nearby Stanley Park, the popular English Bay beach, and many eateries, the area attracted tons of tourists as well as visitors from other areas of the Lower Mainland.

"Your eyes!" Eduardo slapped his hand over his heart. "La violeta. Extraordinario! I have not seen such a shade before. I am professional artista. May I paint you? It would be great honor! You are so be-eau-tiful."

"Thank you." Great honor and beautiful were the

exact words two of the complainants had used in their written statements. "So, how many women have you approached about painting their portraits, especially while riding this bus?"

"Qué?" Eduardo's smile faded. "Why do you ask me this?"

"I'm with Mainland Public Transport security." She showed him her ID card. "We've had harassment complaints about you. One woman threatened to involve the police if it happened again."

His eyes widened. "This cannot be."

"The complaints said you wouldn't take no for an answer until they either changed seats or left the bus."

Eduardo sat back in his seat. "I am stupefied!"

Casey didn't buy the naïve act. "Harassment of any type on MPT buses is against company policy."

He fidgeted, not quite meeting her gaze. "I am just a single man who loves ladies and to create art."

Eduardo produced a business card depicting an elegantly designed maple tree with crimson and tangerine leaves. But anyone could create a card and pass himself off as an artist.

"Is difficult to find models in new city. Art schools are filled up." He frowned. "And many ladies choose to sit next to me and ask what I do to earn money."

She believed him. Given the lusty stares a couple of women were tossing his way, Eduardo had probably found more than a few willing models and dates.

"Is it wrong to talk about art, or to ask a be-eau-tiful lady on a date? I might break bus rules, but I am not breaking real laws, no?"

Casey sighed. "Are you and I going to have a problem?"

He raised his hands, palms facing her. "I do not want trouble, but I must pursue my art."

"Eduardo, the rules are there for a reason. They also give me the authority to kick you off any MPT bus if you're breaking them." Casey paused. "If you're going to discuss portrait painting, then be clear about what you want. If you're turned down, then I strongly advise you to leave the passenger alone. I assume you expect to be paid for your portraits?"

Eduardo nodded. "I do this not only for money but to find true soulmate." He lowered his head. "I am not so lucky in love. Is heartbreaking road filled with big potholes."

"Uh-huh." She studied him. "Do you think you'll find love on a bus?"

"I search everywhere.'"

Eduardo's expression and demeanor seemed sincere, but she had her doubts about this guy.

"You must have tried dating apps," she said.

"Si." He grimaced. "They were not good. Is better to meet ladies in person." He gave her a whimsical look. "Everywhere."

Meaning he intended to keep chatting up women on MPT buses. Eduardo might be better looking and more polite than other rule breakers, but his resistant attitude was all too familiar. She'd be seeing him again, no doubt, and their second encounter wouldn't be as cordial.

"Just be careful about what you say," she cautioned. "Misunderstandings happen easily."

The corners of Eduardo's full, sensuous mouth turned down. "What shall I talk about? The boring weather? Is what others do."

"Eduardo, buddy, unless someone speaks to you first, it might be best if you didn't talk at all."

# TWO

"Lothario Separates Women From Savings." Casey's mouth fell open as she re-read the news story on her phone. An individual known only as Eduardo had allegedly swindled three women out of thousands of dollars. Victims described the suspect as a handsome, thirty-something charmer who'd taken them to lavish restaurants. Within a week, each woman discovered inexplicable charges on her credit card.

The story wasn't from a major outlet and lacked details. It didn't mention his accent or ethnicity or his artistic career. It didn't even say if he'd met the victims on a bus. Unless a more established news source corroborated the info, she wasn't about to call the cops. Besides, she knew where and when to find Eduardo. The bus driver, Lily, had told her that Eduardo rode this route at the same time most evenings.

Seated at the back of the bus in an ankle-length dress, large straw hat, and sunglasses, Casey wanted to avoid his attention this time. One week had passed since she met Eduardo and he was still approaching passengers. Although there'd been no new complaints,

Stan wanted her to monitor the situation and have another chat with Eduardo, should she feel it necessary. If anyone seemed the least bit bothered by Eduardo, Casey was to ask him to leave.

The moment Eduardo entered the bus, Casey drew in a sharp breath. Blue jeans and a black leather jacket were her favorite outfit on a man. Her husband, Lou, often wore similar clothes when he wasn't driving a bus, and it never failed to trigger sparks. Lou wasn't as muscular as Eduardo, but he had plenty of steamy sex appeal. She'd told him about Eduardo. Predictably, Lou was more amused than jealous and thought she should accept Eduardo's offer to paint her portrait.

"I'd love to see a black velvet painting of you in something skimpy," he'd said, wriggling his eyebrows. Casey didn't find the notion as amusing.

Eduardo removed the aviator sunglasses, leaned in, and whispered in Lily's ear as she waited for the final passenger to board. Oh geez, Lily was giggling. In the year Lily had worked for MPT, she and Casey had become friends, but Casey had never seen the level-headed Lily act like that with anyone. She understood the mutual attraction, though. Lily's wavy chestnut hair and smoky gray eyes attracted plenty of admirers, but she also wore wedding rings and kept a professional distance from coworkers and passengers, until now. Lily closed the doors and eased back into traffic.

With a motorcycle helmet tucked under his arm, Eduardo headed down the aisle. Every woman on the bus tracked his movement. Some lifted their purses off the empty seats next to them, yet Eduardo kept going.

He lacked the swagger he had last week. Given what Casey just read, it made sense.

Eduardo spotted her and stared. He then squinted and jutted his chin forward. "Miss Casey?"

So much for incognito. "You recognized me?"

"I study faces for my art." His shoulders relaxed as he sat next to her. "I remember your be-eau-tiful lips and chin. Is delightful to see you again. Have you changed your mind about getting your portrait painted?"

Hmm. Still pushy. "No." She removed her sunglasses. "Where's your motorcycle?"

"My lady friend has one, which we will share."

"Ah." Could be quite the ride. "Have you found any new models this week?"

"No." He seemed to be assessing her. "I do not ask more than once, even though I offer very good deals for portraits. No pressure is what you want, right?"

"It is, and thank you."

"You are welcome." He sat back and looked around before turning back to her. "You are security expert, so you must solve crimes, no?"

"We aren't trained for that. Security personnel only observe and report suspicious activity and occasionally deal with smaller issues. Police do most of the crime-solving." That she'd helped solve a handful of murder investigations over the years wasn't something he needed to know. "Why do you ask?"

"I am curious." He nodded to an admirer gawking at him across the aisle.

The news article suggested it was more than that. Could she learn more? "I guess it's a challenge to earn a living painting portraits."

"Si, but I paint the landscapes, too. There is good market in South America. Customers dream to live in Canada."

"What's your last name?" It wasn't on his business card.

He smiled. "I go by one name, like Cher."

A young woman with long, white-blond dreadlocks sauntered down the aisle and flashed Eduardo a lop-sided grin. Eduardo had been telling Casey about his favorite Vancouver sites when he stopped to wink at the woman. When Lily pulled up to the next stop Eduardo stood up.

"I am grieved to leave you, Miss Casey." He put on his shades. "But I hope we will meet again."

"Maybe. Take care, Eduardo."

If there were no further complaints, she doubted their paths would cross again. Besides, if the fraud news story was true, he'd probably wind up in jail.

As Eduardo sauntered up the aisle, Lily quickly combed her hair, then spritzed it with the travel-sized hairspray she kept in her pocket. They spoke to each other for a few seconds before he left.

After passengers boarded and settled in their seats, Casey approached her. "Eduardo seems to like you."

"We talk whenever he's here late at night." Lily glanced at the mirrors and merged back into traffic.

"What have you learned about him?"

"That he had a rough childhood in Ecuador."

"What happened?"

"Well, when he was five, his father disappeared one

night and never came back. His mom eventually got him and his three sisters to Toronto. Worked two jobs to support the family, but now she has emphysema, so he helps her out financially."

Casey studied her. "He's shared a lot with you."

Lily slowed for the upcoming red light. "I might be the only real friend he has."

Or not. "Is Eduardo as naïve as he sounds or is it just an act?"

Keeping her eyes on the traffic, Lily pinched her lips together. "You think he's a woman-chasing cliché out for as many conquests as he can get."

"Isn't he?"

"No. Look, I get that Eduardo pushes too hard to find models and dates, but he's a romantic guy who truly is looking for a life partner."

Who was being naïve now?

"Maybe Eduardo would have better luck if he acted more naturally," Casey said. "The way he speaks seems kind of fake. How long has he been in Canada?"

"Since he was fifteen." Lily stopped at the red light. "And he's not an idiot, Casey. Just a guy who dropped out of high school to help support his family. Eduardo's only twenty-seven and, yeah, he's immature in a lot of ways, but he has a good heart."

Obviously, the man had won Lily over, but Casey still wasn't convinced. The light turned green and Lily started moving.

"In what way is Eduardo immature?"

"For one thing, he believes he can make a living as an artist in a few years. Based on what he's told me, his mom and sisters did everything for him while he was growing up. Taught him to be respectful and polite to women, especially the older ones. Eduardo was told that if he treated them well, he'd benefit in lots of different ways."

Casey gaped at her. "Are you implying the mom wanted to pimp him out?"

"Not just wanted to, but did, I think." The exit bell rang and Lily slowed the bus. "Eduardo dates a lot of older women. Although he hasn't come right out and said so, I think he's a professional escort."

"Huh." She could be right. "Has he ever asked you for money?"

"Never, but Eduardo did ask to paint my portrait when I first met him." She pulled up to the stop and opened the doors. "He backed off when I told him I have a family to support. In fact, Eduardo insists on paying for coffee and food. One night I told him I'd never gotten flowers for Mother's Day. The next time we met, he brought me a gorgeous bouquet."

"Impressive. And he expected nothing in return?"

"Nope." She watched people enter the bus. "Eduardo just needs a good listener."

"Wouldn't a guy with his looks and manners have plenty of people to talk to?"

"You'd think," Lily remarked, "but men feel threatened by him and most women just want a playmate. Few people see him for who he is."

"And what's that?"

"A lonely young man who misses his family."

Or a sleazy con artist who's scamming women.

# THREE

Another week arrived, along with another complaint about Eduardo. To Casey's surprise, the complainant was Lily this time. For some unknown reason, Eduardo had been texting and leaving her phone messages all Monday and Tuesday, Lily's days off. The guy wanted to know why she'd sent a text Sunday night, begging to see him. Lily insisted she hadn't contacted Eduardo at all, but he wouldn't let it go. Casey didn't know why Lily had given him her cell number in the first place, but that was a question for another time.

As Eduardo boarded, Casey was stunned by his outfit. Did he honestly think the cowboy hat, fringe jacket, and chaps were cool in this city? Eduardo greeted Lily, but she kept her focus on the road.

Eduardo leaned into her. "Lily, I must talk—"

"Sit down or get off the bus," Lily ordered.

He looked taken aback and started to say something but turned away. Spurs jangling, Eduardo headed down the aisle, apparently oblivious to the stares and chuckles.

"Eduardo!" Casey called out. "Have a seat."

"Hola, Miss Casey." Plunking beside her, he scarcely smiled.

"Interesting outfit you're wearing."

"Gracias," he mumbled. "My date loves the cowboys."

Across the aisle, a guy in a muscle shirt and tight shorts ogled Eduardo, who didn't notice. Did Eduardo even realize that the West End was home to people with diverse lifestyles, age groups, and income levels?

"I have big problem, Miss Casey."

No kidding. There'd been two more news reports about the women who'd been scammed by a Hispanic man named Eduardo. How had Eduardo managed to avoid arrest, unless it had already happened and he'd made bail? Not uncommon for white-collar crime charges.

"What's going on?" she asked.

"I was with my good friend Daphne last Sunday," he replied. "After I left, someone murdered her."

"Whoa." Casey sat up straighter. "I saw something about a stabbing on the news. A woman named Daphne Reynard was killed in her home."

"I did not do this horrible thing." Eduardo looked down. "But the policía found my gold satin thong in her bedroom. If they find me, I will be numero uno suspect."

Surveying the passengers, Casey lowered her voice.

"How do you know they found your thong?"

"A friend has sister who is married to policeman. My friend told me about the thong, but it is all wrong. I wore a red sequined one with big yellow flame for Daphne that night. Today, I discover my gold thong is missing. I am being framed up!"

Although Eduardo's anxiety seemed genuine, his story sounded absurd. And did the cop know that his wife had shared information with her brother? Why would she do that unless she was aware that her brother knew Eduardo?

"Did Daphne live alone?" Casey asked.

"Si. She has no children and her husband lives in long-term care home. The housekeeper does not live at Daphne's."

Muscle-shirt guy stood and handed Eduardo a slip of paper. Puzzled, Eduardo read the note as the guy sauntered toward the front exit. At the platform, he blew Eduardo a kiss, then left. Eduardo dropped the note on the floor and kept his expression neutral.

"La policía will also find my DNA in Daphne's bed, yes?"

"Probably, and perhaps fingerprints in the house."

"This is tragic!"

This was nuts. "Eduardo, if someone else killed her, there could be evidence of that person in the house as well."

"There is more." He bit down on his lip. "When I left Daphne's house, I almost knocked over an old man walking his Chihuahua. I was running and did not see him until it was too late."

"Why were you running?"

"Another lady friend sent urgent text, saying she was in great danger and needed me to come urgently. Daphne was in happy sleep, so I left."

Was this the text he thought Lily sent? "Did your friend say what kind of danger she was in?"

"I asked, but she did not reply. I was very worried."

"Maybe I should talk to her. What's her name?"

I cannot tell you. I promised to keep it secret."

It had to be Lily. "Did you take a bus to get there?"

"For Daphne, I always rent a car. It was parked in front of neighbor's house."

Too bad he hadn't taken a bus. Any driver would remember a guy with Eduardo's looks, but how would a struggling artist find the money to rent a car, unless he really was a professional escort?

"What happened when you met your friend?"

"She did not show up and now she insists she did not send the text. I am puzzled beyond belief!" His eyes were intense. "I would not harm any of my ladies. I do not know what to do."

"Any of your ladies?" Lily's theory about his work had to be correct. "Eduardo, I'm sorry if this sounds too personal, but are you a professional escort, by any chance?"

He studied her for several seconds. "Si. I do not earn enough from painting, so I have other jobs." His expression brightened. "I was hired to perform with an exotic dance crew two months ago. The tips are fantástico."

Good grief. Well, that explained where the cowboy costume came from. "You're a stripper, too?"

"Is honest work, Miss Casey, like painting or escorting ladies to dinner or concerts."

What about dishonest work, like scamming women?

"Do you, by any chance, have access to your ladies' credit cards when you're paid for escorting?"

Eduardo's brow creased. "Why do you ask this?"

After Casey showed him one of the news articles on her phone, beads of sweat appeared on his forehead.

"I heard about this story." Eduardo removed a tissue from his pocket and dabbed the perspiration. "I wished to tell you last time but was afraid you'd think I was lying. I would never steal from my ladies. It is also a frameup."

Maybe. Maybe not. "Have the police talked to you about these women?"

"No."

But they would. "Who'd want to set you up?"

"I think it is one of the dancers. I kept my gold satin thong in locker at work." Eduardo peered at her. "I will hire you to find out which one did it."

"Sorry Eduardo, but I'm not qualified and don't have the time anyway. I could give you the names of a couple of private investigators."

"But I know you." Eduardo clasped his hands together. "I will not survive prison. I am ladies' man, not man's man. Please help me, señorita."

"Actually, I'm a happily married señora."

"Ah." Eduardo nodded. "Pretending is necessary sometimes, no? When Daphne and I were together, we would pretend to be perfect couple."

Casey cringed. She didn't want any details. "Do you know if she went out with other men, or had any conflicts with people in her life?"

Eduardo shook his head. "Daphne was compassionate lady who worked with many charities."

Casey glanced at the passengers, relieved that most of them were too absorbed with their phones to be eavesdropping.

"Eduardo, who knew you'd be seeing Daphne on Sunday night?"

"I told no one. I do not work for escort service and make my own dates. No one except you knows I do this. My ladies expect privacy." Eduardo blinked a couple of times as if thinking this over. "But the dancers all knew Daphne. She did not care about secrecy. Daphne came to the shows and gave me generous tips. The other guys were jealous, I could tell."

"Which one of them could have gotten into your locker?"

"Everyone," Eduardo murmured. "We leave lockers open for fast costume changes." He pulled out his phone. "You should come to show and talk to those guys. Here is the address."

"I doubt they'd talk to me. Maybe you should call the police before they find you."

"No! They will not listen to someone like me." Eduardo shook his head. "I will be arrested."

He had a point. "You've dug yourself a deep hole, my friend."

"Si." Eduardo grimaced. "I am not good climber."

What if Eduardo was innocent? Mrs. Reynard's Point Grey home sat on some of the most expensive real estate in Canada. A woman who lived alone in a multimillion-dollar property could attract nasty gold diggers.

Lily pulled up to the next stop and started talking on her cell. She wasn't supposed to use her phone even when stopped. So, what was going on?

"Eduardo, when did you get the text from your

friend on Sunday night?"

"Fifteen minutes before twelve, but I did not see it till midnight. When I did, I left right away and drove to the diner where we always meet."

Lily glanced over her shoulder, met Casey's gaze, and continued her phone conversation. Casey raised her eyebrows, but Lily ended her call and resumed driving.

"Do you recall what time you arrived at the diner?" Casey asked.

"Twenty past twelve, but my friend was not there. She did not answer texts or phone. I waited till one o'clock, then left." Eduardo glanced at Lily. "I think my friend is afraid of trouble."

No doubt. Management wouldn't be thrilled if Lily was drawn into a murder trial involving a man she'd befriended on the job. MPT expected exemplary behavior from employees. Casey wouldn't put it past company president Gwyn Maddox to decide that Lily had crossed a professional line and either suspend or fire her. Was this a good enough reason for Lily to lie about a text?

Eduardo's phone rang. "Oh!" He smiled as he answered. "Thank you for calling. I am so happy."

Although Lily had her back to Casey, she was clearly on the phone again, and driving, which was illegal. Something was definitely wrong. She suspected that Eduardo was talking to Lily, but why would Lily call him now?

"I will be getting off at Waterfront Station, then catching SeaBus," Eduardo said to his caller. "We can talk later tonight, yes?"

He was talking to Lily all right, but why would she ask where he was headed? Waterfront Station was a major transit hub less than ten minutes away. It was also home to the SeaBus that transported passengers across the harbor to North Vancouver. Casey noted their surroundings. They'd be turning onto Burrard Street soon. From there it was a short drive north to Waterfront Station.

"Bueno." Eduardo hung up and smiled.

Lily turned the corner, then eased the bus to another stop.

"Good news?" Casey asked, aware that Lily now appeared to be texting someone. Her stomach fluttered and she couldn't shake the uneasiness.

"Si. I think things will be better, Miss Casey."

"Oh?" When he didn't respond to her question, she added, "You sound positive."

"My mother taught me to believe in love and miracles and good things in life." He beamed. "That is why art is so be-eau-tiful, Miss Casey. It creates light from darkness and offers hope of great possibilities. Art is freer of truths."

"Freer of truths?" She tried not to smile. "I'm not sure I follow."

Eduardo's eyes shone. "Art exposes who we truly are. The secret parts of ourselves. Is complicated but also simple. I do not know enough English to explain better."

Eduardo's passion for his art was obvious. "I think you explained it well."

As soon as Lily pulled up to Waterfront Station,

Eduardo stood and said, "I must depart, now. Buenas noches, Miss Casey."

"Take care, Eduardo."

The man had barely stepped off the platform before he was surrounded by four police officers with weapons drawn.

Through the open windows, she heard one of them yell, "On the ground now! Hands behind your head!"

"But this is new outfit!" As Eduardo scrambled back onto the platform, his phone fell out of his shirt pocket, landing near Lily. "Lily! Read the text!" he shouted. "Password is backward numbers!"

Lily slipped the phone into her pocket while Casey jogged up the aisle. Two officers grabbed Eduardo from behind and dragged him off the platform. By the time Casey reached the front and peered outside, Eduardo was face down on the sidewalk and his wrists were being restrained behind his back. He was hauled to his feet. It troubled Casey to see his shoulders rounded and head lowered in utter defeat. She turned to Lily whose complexion had turned bright pink.

"Were your phone calls about Eduardo, Lily? Did you know this was coming?"

Lily glanced at the passengers who were now watching the activity outside. "Dispatch called and said the cops got a report about a man in a cowboy costume at a bus stop. They said he was carrying a knife and threatening to kill passengers once he boarded. I told them it couldn't be true. That Eduardo rides this bus all the time and has never shown any violent tendencies. I also made it clear that he was happily chatting with you."

"What did dispatch say?"

"That the cops needed to follow up anyway. They asked if I knew which stop he might exit, so I told them maybe you could find out."

Casey sighed. "Why did you do that?"

"Because I don't want them to know that he and I are friends." She hesitated. "I called Eduardo and he told me, but I had no idea they'd treat him so badly."

"Lily, you could have just said you had no idea where he was going and left it at that."

"Sorry," she mumbled. "But they were putting me on the spot and I thought you could help. You're way better at handling awkward situations than I am."

Casey overheard snippets of conversation outside, including the words homicide suspect. Eduardo was in serious trouble. But how would these cops know of his connection to the victim so quickly unless somebody told them?

"They think Eduardo might have killed someone," Casey said.

"What?" Her eyes widened. "That's insane."

"You didn't see the news? A woman was murdered in her Point Grey home on Sunday night. Eduardo told me he was with her just before she died."

"I don't watch the news and he never said a word about it."

Casey edged closer and whispered, "If Eduardo tells them about the text he thinks you sent, you'll probably hear from the cops and his lawyer."

The color in Lily's cheeks bloomed several shades darker. "But I didn't see Eduardo that night and I don't know the victim."

"News sources say that Daphne Reynard died between midnight and 2:00 AM. You were driving this route and your shift finished at one. So, the lawyer might try to use the text as Eduardo's alibi, which puts you in the middle of things."

Lily clamped her hand over her mouth. Winding up in court would be not only embarrassing for a woman with a young son and a husband, but dangerous if the killer didn't want her corroborating Eduardo's alibi, if she even could. What if Eduardo wasn't innocent?

"Casey, I swear I didn't send the text."

She seemed sincere, which only made things more confusing. "Okay, Lily. Maybe you should look at his phone and see what's going on."

Lily removed Eduardo's iPhone from her pocket. "He said his password was backward numbers." She glanced at the passengers. "Could you do it? I'm behind schedule and people are starting to glare at me."

"Sure."

While Lily closed the door and waited for the traffic to clear, Casey typed in 6-5-4-3-2-1 and got in. Man, if Eduardo was that careless about passwords, what else was he careless about? Casey scrolled down his list of messages. She spotted one from Lily, dated the night of the murder. *I need 2 C U! Pls come to diner! I'm in serious danger!* Casey showed it to her.

"That can't be." Lily groaned and shook her head. "This is a nightmare!"

"The text was sent fifteen minutes before twelve. Eduardo reached the diner at twenty past twelve and waited for you until one."

"This is a huge mistake." Lily eased away from the curb. "Eduardo's not capable of murder."

"Yet, I'm here because he was bothering you."

"Because it was so out of character for him."

A vehicle cut her off and Lily hit the brakes. Casey grabbed the pole right behind Lily's seat and steadied herself.

"I just wanted Eduardo to stop talking about the bloody text," Lily added. Her lips were pinched, eyes blinking at the road.

"Lily, I don't mean to pry," Casey murmured, "but why all the chats with Eduardo in the first place? What was in it for you?"

Lily watched the traffic. "Frank's been miserable to live with lately and, well, Eduardo's a good listener." Her smoky eyes flashed at Casey. "We're not having an affair, if that's what you're wondering. Though I admit I've thought about it."

"Okay." She'd been wondering how far Lily had taken things. "I guess you didn't see the news reports about a handsome Hispanic man who's been accused of fraud?"

"No. Why?"

"The victims, all women, said the man was named Eduardo. He allegedly took them out on dates and stole their credit card numbers."

Lily swore under her breath. "It's not him."

"How can you be so sure?"

"Because it contradicts everything I know about the guy."

Lily hadn't known Eduardo long, though. What if

he excelled at lying?

"If you helped prove his innocence," Lily went on, "then maybe my name could be left out of it."

"The cops won't want me meddling in their investigation."

"You're making an excuse." Lily's mouth twisted with disdain. "I saw the derision on your face when you were talking with Eduardo tonight. You haven't changed your mind about him one bit. To you, he's still a shallow stereotype taking advantage of women."

"Did you know he was a stripper?"

She avoided Casey's gaze. "I thought you'd judge him even more harshly and refuse to see the kind, vulnerable man he is."

Was Lily that astute or that gullible? The exit bell rang and she slowed for the next stop.

"His lawyer will help him, Lily."

"I doubt he even has one, and let's be real. An uneducated, visible minority won't get the best lawyer and the cops won't look for other suspects." Lily pulled up to the stop. As she opened the doors, she turned to Casey. "Everyone knows you're an excellent investigator who's gone out of her way to help others."

The flattery card. Really?

"Eduardo doesn't know many people, so it wouldn't be hard to find out who's trying to destroy his life," Lily added. "Can you do this for me before the cops show up at my door and my life blows up? I honestly don't know anything about the murder and fraud. I can't be involved in this, Casey." She gasped for air. "I just can't!"

"Lily, calm down." The poor woman was starting to

hyperventilate. "Take a deep breath."

Once Lily got herself under control, Casey said, "Before I do anything, I need to ask you something."

Lily closed the doors and checked the mirrors.

"What is it?"

"Are there texts between you and Eduardo that would establish a relationship?"

Lily's jaw clenched as she eased the bus back into traffic. "If Frank finds out about me and Eduardo's friendship, I'm in deep shit." Her voice caught. "Our marriage is—Well, there's some crap going on. This isn't the time to get into it."

Casey felt bad for Lily, but prying into Eduardo's life could get them both in trouble. "I'm going to leave soon and catch another bus back to MPT. Let's talk tomorrow."

Keeping her eyes on the road, Lily handed Eduardo's phone to her. "Please take this. I don't want to be near it."

Casey didn't think she should, but Lily's eyes were wild, her anxiety way too high. "I'll take it to lost-and-found in the morning."

Casey returned to her seat, puzzling over their discussion. If Lily had told the truth about not sending the text, then someone else must have used her phone. She highly doubted it was her husband, Frank. He would have been taking care of their son that night. Even if he'd already seen the texts between her and Eduardo and had been furious over it, he wouldn't know about Eduardo's date with Daphne. The theory didn't make sense.

Casey peeked at Eduardo's calendar, which was filled with the first names of women, restaurants, and entertainment venues. Eduardo might not be a genius, but was he so dumb that he'd use his real name in a fraud scheme or leave incriminating evidence at a crime scene? That didn't make sense either.

A quick scroll through his messages showed that Eduardo had been in contact with at least six women this week. Daphne Reynard was the one he'd texted most.

Casey looked out the window. Reading personal messages between Daphne and Eduardo didn't feel right, never mind the ones between him and Lily. She'd hold off until Lily had a chance to tell her more. Besides, she needed to give Stan a call. He always wanted to be briefed on unusual events right away. Lily's role in Eduardo's arrest certainly qualified on that score.

# FOUR

Casey corrected typos in the incident report Stan requested last night, then pushed her chair back and stretched. She glanced at the four empty desks in MPT's cramped security department. Stan's secretary had already left for lunch and other security team members were either off today or on the buses. The far end of the long, rectangular room occupied by accounting and HR personnel was also empty. Stan's closed door meant he didn't want interruptions, so she was alone.

Casey opened her desk drawer and removed Eduardo's phone. She stared at the case depicting a smiling avocado with googly eyes and stick arms and legs. Not the type of phone case most men would choose, but Eduardo wasn't like most men. She'd left his phone in her locker last night and planned to take it to lost-and-found once she finished the report.

Why hadn't Lily called her or even returned a short response to her texts? Casey's messages made it clear she needed to talk to her as soon as possible. Had something happened or was Lily simply avoiding her?

Casey had been weighing the pros and cons of

browsing through texts between her and Eduardo. If Lily wanted help in staying out of Eduardo's legal mess, then Casey needed to know what was going on with the urgent text sent to Eduardo. So, what to do? Casey sat back, stared at the phone, and decided. After typing Eduardo's password, she scrolled through his messages to Lily.

Thankfully, nothing sexual appeared to be going on between them. They often asked how each other was doing and arranged to meet on her breaks, but that was it. So, why wouldn't Lily confide in her?

Casey placed Eduardo's phone back in the drawer and called her cop friend, Denver Davies. She missed taking criminology classes with him, but Denver had lost interest in moving up Vancouver Police Department's career ladder. These days, he seemed happy to remain a patrol officer. Despite hair-raising encounters with the darker side of humanity, Denver hadn't lost his compassion or his sense of humor.

"It's been a while, Casey," he said. "How are classes going?"

"Slowly. I'm taking the summer off," she answered. "Can I ask your help with something?"

"You can always ask, but I'm not sure how helpful I'll be."

After she explained what she knew about Eduardo's situation and the possibility that he was being set up for murder, Casey said, "I sat next to him last night, Denver, and he wasn't carrying a knife or threatening anyone. Something's really off here. I mean, why would the cops even think of Eduardo as a homicide suspect at that point unless his fingerprints were in the system? DNA analysis takes time, so I was wondering if you could find out who phoned in the tip about him. If it's anonymous, wouldn't it back up Eduardo's claim?"

"Not necessarily. Listen, I'm at home right now, working evenings these days, but let me check into it."

"No problem, and thanks."

Casey went back to work. By the time she'd edited her report once more and printed it out, Denver called back.

"You were right about the caller's anonymity. The number was untraceable, probably a burner, so I asked around and learned a couple of things," he said. "First, fingerprints were found at the crime scene, but they didn't match anyone in the system. They do match Eduardo Ruiz, however."

So, that was his last name. "What else?"

"I wanted to know who found the victim's body. It turns out that first responders did, thanks to an anonymous tip about a dark-haired man seen running from the property around midnight. The male caller said he'd seen him at the house a few times and had heard rumors that he worked as a male stripper."

"Oh, boy," Casey murmured. Two phone tips and a gold satin thong had led the cops straight to Eduardo. "Looks like Eduardo's made an enemy."

"The investigating officers will find out. Anything else they should know?"

If she told him what Eduardo said about his thong at the crime scene, a cop could find himself in trouble for leaking info. Best to stay out of it.

"Casey? Your silence tells me you're holding something back."

She forgot that intuitiveness was one of Denver's strong suits. "I've read news stories about a credit card scam. Women were targeted by a Hispanic man named Eduardo. But he insists this is part of the setup. Do you know if Eduardo's also been charged with fraud?"

"Second-degree murder," Denver answered. "Don't get involved, okay? Helping Ruiz could lead you to places you don't want to go."

"I know, but I'm more worried about one of our drivers, Lily, who's a friend of mine. She and Eduardo have had coffee together a few times and she's afraid she could be dragged into his mess. Lily has a husband and young son, Denver."

"Okay, but how would she be dragged into this?"

If anyone else had asked, she wouldn't say a word, but Denver had just done her a favor and she trusted him not to exploit private conversations.

"Eduardo received a text from her the night of the murder, but Lily insists she didn't send it."

"Any idea what it said?"

Casey took a breath and recited what she'd memorized. "It was sent at quarter to twelve, and Lily was driving that night, on a route in Eduardo's neighborhood. Her shift ended at one."

"I see." He paused. "Helping people in dicey situations has hurt you before, so like I said, please stay out of this."

Stan opened his door.

"Noted, and thanks for the info." She ended the call as Stan approached. "Finished lunch already?"

"Such as it was," he grumbled. "Nora's got me on a low-fat diet with smaller portion sizes. I'll be starving in an hour."

Stan was a beefy guy anyway, so she hadn't noticed the extra pounds. Far more noticeable was another poor wardrobe choice. Today's getup was a mauve dress shirt, tomato-red tie, and brown cargo pants. Nora once told Casey that he only let her choose his clothes for special occasions. Clearly, work wasn't that special.

"Have you finished your report?" Stan asked.

"Just printed it off."

The sound of a mariachi band erupted from her drawer.

Stan raised an eyebrow. "New ringtone?"

"Not my phone." Casey opened the drawer and muted the noise. "It's Eduardo's. I'm going to take it to lost-and-found."

"The guy who was busted?" Stan gave her one of his measured stares. "What if something in that phone implicates him? Maybe the cops should have it."

"Eduardo yelled out the password as he was being hauled away. Hardly the action of a man with something to hide. Lily doesn't believe he killed anyone and asked me to help prove his innocence."

Stan frowned. "But he's been harassing her."

Unless she had to, Casey didn't want to share the content of a private text with an MPT executive. If Stan thought Lily's texts with a passenger implicated her or MPT in a potential legal issue, Lily would definitely wind up in hot water with her supervisors, not to mention Gwyn.

"There's been a misunderstanding they both want to sort out."

"So, do you think the guy's innocent?"

"I can't say for sure, but something's not adding up. Anyhow, I don't want Lily caught in his legal troubles."

"How could that happen?"

Uh-oh. How to phrase this without landing in quicksand? "When Lily first came to us about the complaint, remember her saying that Eduardo had been friendly and chatty up to that point?"

"I do."

"Well, what if he told her things that would interest the cops? They could wind up coming here to question Lily or go to her home, which would upset her."

Stan rubbed his forehead. "This just keeps getting better and better."

His ringtone, "Friends in Low Places," blared from Stan's back pocket. Based on his responses and the deepening lines on his forehead, he was being summoned to a meeting he didn't want to attend. Casey held her breath, hoping he'd have to leave so he wouldn't ask any more questions, at least for now.

When Stan's call ended, he said, "I'll be back in an hour. But think long and hard before you involve yourself in Lily's business, and I need to have a chat with her."

You and me both, she thought. "I can't let a friend down, Stan."

"I know, kiddo, and I'm counting on you not to send any legal hassles our way."

The moment he left the room, Casey checked Eduardo's phone. The call had come from someone named MC. *Sorry I missed your call. Call me.* Casey found MC's number in his contact list. A quick reverse directory search revealed that MC was short for Man Cave. More keystrokes brought up a web page depicting half-naked men flaunting six-packs and super-sized biceps. Eduardo posed in a matador's costume minus the shirt. It looked like Man Cave was the name of the troupe Eduardo performed with. Someone from work had called him.

"Whoo boy! If you're going to a show, count me in," a familiar voice said from behind her. "I heard that those guys are spectacular."

Marie Crenshaw leaned over Casey's shoulder and ogled the screen. Casey's coworker had never been shy about inviting herself anywhere or going after what she wanted.

"I haven't thought about it."

"Well, you should."

The webpage highlighted the Friday and Saturday showtimes. The troupe was in Vancouver only two more weeks before heading to Calgary. If she did see the show, she'd bring her best friend, Kendal Winters. Kendal's work as a loss prevention officer at a department store had taught her to assess people quickly. Interviewing these guys would be Kendal's idea of a dream job.

"Come on, Casey." Marie smacked her shoulder. "Have some fun."

Casey's gaze drifted over the six-packs. Maybe

checking a couple of things out on Lily's behalf wouldn't be so terrible. She'd have a drink, watch the show, then chat with a couple of strippers. What could possibly go wrong?

# FIVE

Randy the Handy Man dropped his tool belt on the floor and gyrated his hips.

"Whoa." Casey's eyes widened.

Kendal nudged her. "Like the way his jeans show every bulge?" She grinned. "A lot to take in, huh? Like *huge*."

Casey fanned herself with a brochure. Man, it was hot in here and not just from the lusty performances. She'd been cocooned in this stuffy, two-hundred-seat room for over two hours and the place was sizzling in every way imaginable. Women were shouting and cheering. A few were so drunk they couldn't stand up without grabbing onto something or someone.

To Casey's chagrin, Marie was one of the plastered spectators. She'd overheard Casey arrange a time with Kendal and insisted on tagging along. Since Marie sucked at keeping secrets, Casey hadn't mentioned coming here to gather info about Eduardo's coworkers.

"Take it off!" Marie shouted at Randy. She removed her stilettos and made a wobbly attempt to stand on her chair.

"Marie, stop!" Casey grabbed her arm. "You'll hurt yourself."

With a quick snap, Randy tore off his jeans. The crowd roared. Kendal—a statuesque blonde with a long reach—waved a five-dollar bill at Handy Randy, who shimmied toward her. Kendal slipped the money into the waistband of his denim bikini briefs. The audience went nuts. Randy turned and wiggled his taut butt in Kendal's face. Women pounded the tables and yelled things that would make most men blush.

"Look at her, throwing money around!" Marie shouted in Casey's ear. "The woman's desperate for attention."

Casey wasn't about to admit that this was her and Kendal's plan. Kendal thought it'd be fun to convince the dancers she was so rich that they'd do anything to accommodate her, like answer a few questions. To play her role, she wore a stunning red dress and her mom's diamond necklace, earrings, and rings.

"What did you say Kendal does for a living?" Marie asked.

"She's a loss prevention officer."

"It must pay better than I thought."

Casey smiled. "Normally, she's quite frugal."

Both Marie and Kendal had big personalities and even bigger mouths. Although they hadn't met before tonight, Kendal knew enough about Casey's professional rivalry with Marie, as well as an old personal rivalry over Lou, to make it clear she didn't like Marie. Marie picked up on it pretty quick and threw the attitude right back.

"You're fabulous!" Kendal told Randy.

"Back at ya, sweetheart."

Kendal was enjoying her role, and why not? She was single and loved a good time. With luck, her generosity would motivate at least one of them to talk about a particular performer known as Sexy Samurai Danny. Casey had gotten the lead after a phone call with Eduardo's lawyer this afternoon.

The lawyer had tracked down her work number in an effort to contact Lily. Eduardo couldn't remember Lily's number and wanted his phone back. After telling him where the phone was, Casey asked the lawyer to find out from Eduardo which troupe member resented him most. Two hours later, the lawyer gave her Danny's name. Samurai Danny also happened to be Randy the Handy Man's brother.

Apparently, Danny wanted to become the show's headliner for the extra pay and prestige, but the show's manager was considering Eduardo for the role. Personally, Casey hadn't enjoyed Danny's cheesy sword routine. He'd received his share of shouts, whistles, and applause, though. She wanted to know what the crew thought of him and his grudge against Eduardo.

Mercifully, Randy was the evening's last dancer. Strobing lights and blaring music were giving Casey a headache. When Randy's number ended, the crowd rose and stomped their feet, demanding an encore. Randy blew kisses and waved, then knelt in front of Kendal and whispered something in her ear. Kendal nodded and watched him jog off the stage.

"He's asked us to stick around," she told Casey.

"Awesome!" Marie hiccupped.

Casey gave her a stern look. "I need you to be cool, okay?"

"No prob." Marie plunked in her chair and began searching for her shoes.

With the last curtain call, all seven men swaggered onto the stage. Strobe lights bounced around the room in a nauseating frenzy while the audience screamed and lost their minds. After the guys displayed their trademark moves, they lined up and took a bow. The four younger men were slightly thinner and shorter than the three hulks in their thirties, but all were deeply tanned.

As the troupe left the stage, Danny gave his brother Randy a push. Randy stumbled into the curtain but kept going without acknowledging the gesture. Casey glanced at Kendal who returned a quizzical look.

The music ended and the houselights came on. Two women started up some steps at the far corner of the stage until a bouncer blocked them. Reluctantly, they turned and joined the exiting stream.

"Looks like we'll have to wait for Randy to come to us," Casey remarked.

"That shove didn't look friendly," Kendal replied.

"I want to meet the hotties." Marie bounced up and down. "Let's go on a manhunt!"

Casey groaned. "I thought you were going to play it cool."

"Hey, I wasn't the one waving cash at thrusting pelvises," she retorted. "I'm surprised Kendal didn't toss her panties, too." Marie flung back her thick red hair and marched toward the steps, where the bouncer stood with his hands on his hips and stared her down.

"You realize that bringing her here was a horrible

idea, right?" Kendal said.

"Yep."

Marie was arguing with the bouncer when Randy appeared and said something to him. The bouncer vanished behind the curtain as Casey and Kendal joined Marie.

"Did you ladies enjoy the show?"

"Totally!" Marie gushed, climbing the stairs. "You're amazing!"

Randy glanced at the crew, who were putting the equipment away. "We're not allowed to take guests backstage, but I was hoping to buy you all a drink. There's lots of great places within walking distance."

"We'd love that," Kendal answered.

Casey wasn't so sure. Marie was in no shape to sit down and quietly listen to their conversation. Even if she could, she'd want to know why Casey was asking about Samurai Danny. On the other hand, this was her one chance to learn something useful enough to pass along to the cops.

"Are the other dancers as friendly as you?" Casey asked, opening the club's glossy pamphlet. "Maybe you could introduce us to a couple of them."

"Sorry, but most of the guys have partners to get home to, and the rest have other engagements."

"What about this one?" Casey pointed to Eduardo. She'd almost lost it when she read that his stage name was Don Juan Dong. "We didn't see him tonight."

Randy gave them a wry smile. "Just between us, he's a little weird. Probably called in sick."

"Hello, lovely ladies." Danny sauntered up to them

and zeroed in on Kendal.

Casey's body stiffened. It wasn't just Eduardo's opinion about him that bothered her, or his cheesy performance, or even the way he'd shoved his brother. It was the intensity swirling around him. Randy's smile had disappeared altogether. Casey noticed the lines on both men's faces beneath their makeup. Easily in their mid-thirties or older.

"Hi, ya," Marie said to Danny. "Loved your Samurai routine."

"Thanks." He flicked back his long black hair and winked at his brother's stony expression.

Casey wondered how competitive the brothers were with each other. She wouldn't be surprised if they'd been that way most of their lives.

A pudgy man in a wrinkled suit marched up to them. "My apologies, ladies, but you'll have to head outside. We're closing the doors soon."

"I take it you're the manager?" Kendal asked.

"I am." His gaze lingered on her diamonds. "Call me RJ. I hope you enjoyed the show."

Kendal grinned. "We sure did."

"Excellent." RJ's phone rang, and he stepped behind the curtain.

"Unfortunately, I have an appointment," Danny said, his attention on Kendal, "but my brother'll be happy to buy you a drink." He tapped Randy's shoulder. "Hope to see you again soon."

"Can't wait." Marie practically swooned toward him.

As Danny hurried off, the performer known as the Hawaiian Hottie joined them. Still wearing only a loincloth, the guy sported intricate symmetrical patterns and designs tattooed over much of his massive body. Casey spotted a sun, turtle shell, and exquisitely designed cross.

Randy swept his bangs back and grunted. It seemed he wasn't happy with the guy's appearance either.

"Aloha," he said, ignoring Randy. "Would anyone like a special backstage tour?"

"Me!" Marie gripped his oversize bicep and ran her hand down his arm. "You are the most decorative man I've ever seen, like a live painting."

"I thought we weren't allowed back there," Casey said.

"The manager just went into his office and shut the door," he replied. "We'll be quick."

"Cool." Marie swooned.

"Maybe you should stay with us," Casey said.

"Brian?" Randy's jaw tightened. "Are you sure that's a good idea?"

The Hawaiian waved his hand dismissively. "We'll be back in less than ten minutes." Without waiting for a response, he and Marie vanished behind the curtain.

Randy's mouth twitched as if he wanted to speak, but he kept silent.

"Everything all right?" Casey asked.

He seemed reluctant to answer. "Your friend strikes me as the type who knows her mind."

"She is." Casey's concern rose. "Is Marie safe with him?"

Randy rubbed his jaw. "Brian's a lover, not a fighter. If she was in danger from anyone in the alley, he'd protect her, no question."

Yet, something seemed to be troubling him. "Maybe we should—"

"There's a great pub next door," Randy interrupted, turning to Kendal, "and other places nearby."

While he and Kendal chatted, Casey checked the time. Five minutes had passed since Marie left. Casey tapped her foot until RJ reappeared, his pudgy face scowling.

"Our Hawaiian performer just took your friend into the alley behind the building. Better fetch her right away. Randy, escort our guests down the hall, *now*." He spotted two guys stacking equipment and yelled, "Hey, not like that!" RJ stomped toward them.

"Why's your manager so angry about Brian taking our friend outside?" Kendal asked.

"Because of what usually happens out there," Randy answered. "Brian promised to behave after a video of one of his dalliances went viral." He led them toward a set of stairs. "It's why we call him Back-Alley Brian."

Kendal and Casey exchanged horrified glances.

"She wouldn't, wouldn't she?" Kendal asked Casey. "Wait. What am I saying? Of course, she would."

Casey groaned. "Afraid so."

"Worst idea ever, Casey."

"Yeah, thanks, Kendal," she grumbled. "Got it."

"This way," Randy said, gesturing toward a wooden staircase.

Gripping the railing, they followed him down the steps, through another door, then along a narrow, concrete hallway illuminated by three bare bulbs. Glancing through an open door on her right, Casey spotted a younger man wearing dress pants and a suit vest over a pink dress shirt with the sleeves rolled up. The guy was too thin and gangly to be a stripper. Sporting a fedora tilted at an angle, his face was partially concealed as he talked to Danny.

Casey passed a second open door on the right, near the exit, exposing a cluttered dressing room. Randy opened the exit. She hurried outside and froze.

It was tough to say what was worse, the stench of rotting garbage from two overloaded dumpsters or the site of Marie and Hawaiian Brian making out between the dumpsters.

"Marie!" Casey yelled, marching up to her. "Time to go!"

Marie pulled away and peeked around his body. "I'm not finished!"

"Yes, you are."

"Brian?" Randy called out from the doorway. "RJ knows."

The Hawaiian spun around. "You told him?"

"He saw you."

Brian gave him a long stare as if he didn't believe him. Casey glowered at the sleazy Hawaiian stomping toward the back door without giving Marie a second glance.

"You ruined my evening!" Marie ran her hands through her hair, which was now all kinks and bobbles frayed in every direction.

"Really, Marie?" Casey plunked her hands on her hips. "Maybe you'd think otherwise if you weren't so wasted."

"I'm not that bad, and I'm single and can do what I

want."

"She's also forty years old with three ex-husbands," Kendal remarked. "Not some naïve little miss."

"I'm thirty-nine! Is that what Casey told you? That I'm forty?"

"*That's* your takeaway from this? A miscalculation about age?" Kendal rolled her eyes.

Marie hiccupped again. "Where's the bathroom?"

"Inside, first door on your right," Randy said, his expression impassive.

Marie teetered forward and fell, smacking her knees on the gritty, cracked asphalt. Casey and Kendal helped her get back on her feet. The floodlight over the door exposed scrapes and trickling blood.

"That was close," Marie mumbled. "Could of hurt myself."

"You did, you moron. Better wash it out to avoid infection," Kendal replied.

Marie either didn't hear her or was ignoring her.

"You don't feel anything?" Casey asked.

"Well, nothing bad," she answered with a smirk.

Randy was still holding the door open as they made their way toward him. Since Marie could barely walk in those spiked heels without assistance, the trek felt painfully long.

"Sorry, Randy, but we'll have to take a rain check on that drink," Casey said. "I'm going to drive my friend home."

His jaw tightened. "That's too bad, but I get it." He turned to Kendal. "If you give me your number, we can arrange another time."

"Absolutely."

"Let me get my phone." He hurried into the dressing room across from the bathroom.

While Marie washed up, Casey whispered, "You aren't giving him your cell number, are you?"

"Work number. Since you didn't get what you came for, we might need to see him again."

Casey wasn't sure she wanted to.

Fedora guy emerged from the room at the other end of the hall and started toward the exit, his focus on his phone. Angry shouts erupted behind a door marked Manager. Fedora guy glanced at it, then picked up the pace as Randy reappeared in the hallway. The two men nearly collided yet didn't acknowledge each other, which seemed a little strange to Casey.

Randy tapped the number Kendal recited into his phone and said, "I'd better go. If RJ catches me with you here, I'll get an earful, too." He stared at the door. "Looks like Brian just blew his chance at becoming a headliner."

"Is that what he wants?" Casey asked.

"It's what most of the guys want. Better pay and tons of publicity, solo engagements, and other perks. Right now, he'll be lucky if he can keep this gig."

Randy returned to the dressing room as Marie emerged from the bathroom, her hair less messy and the lipstick smears around her mouth gone.

"Come on, Cinderella," Kendal said. "Time to go home before your stilettos turn into tattered bunny slippers."

"Stuff it."

Kendal muttered something unintelligible.

"Marie's extra snarky whenever things don't go her way," Casey murmured. "Especially when she's had too much to drink."

Kendal grimaced. "Charming."

Outside, Marie again stumbled over the asphalt. This time, Casey and Kendal caught her before she hit the ground. Casey grunted from the extra weight. Her coworker was no delicate doily. At least the parking lot was beside the building.

"I don't suppose your Hawaiian said anything interesting about the club or his colleagues?" Casey asked.

"His tongue was busy elsewhere," Marie replied, "which you busybodies ruined."

Kendal rolled her eyes. "Listen up, you middle-aged degenerate. We just kept you from committing an indecent act in public and are trying to protect you from a total face-plant on filthy asphalt. You're a mess."

"I'll be fine," Marie mumbled, swaying.

Casey wondered about that, since Marie had three teenagers to face at home.

# SIX

Casey pulled the comforter over her head and tried to ignore her ringing phone. When it finally stopped, she peeked out and squinted at the clock radio. Nine-thirty already? Normally, she didn't sleep in this late, but last night's adventure had left her so exhausted that she didn't even hear Lou get ready for work. Today, she needed to catch up on MPT paperwork. Stan often worked Saturday mornings for the same reason, but he wouldn't expect her to show up early.

Yawning, she reached for the phone and listened to a message from Eduardo's lawyer. A judge had granted Eduardo bail and he'd be coming by MPT to pick up his phone this afternoon. A lawyer and bail already? Fast work.

After showering and dressing, she returned his call.

"I'm glad Eduardo's out, but a little surprised, given the seriousness of the charge."

"It helps that my client has no criminal record or a history of drug and alcohol abuse," the lawyer answered. "Even more helpful is that one of Mrs. Reynard's neighbors spotted two men at her house that night."

"Ah. Any idea who the other man is?"

"The description's vague. We're hoping they'll find more evidence."

"Will Eduardo be charged with fraud?"

"Not without solid proof, which doesn't exist because my client didn't do it. So, when can Eduardo collect his phone?"

Direct and clearly on team Eduardo. She liked that.

"Our lost-and-found department's open till five."

"Eduardo's with me and he'd like to talk to you," the lawyer said. "I'll put you on speakerphone."

"Hola, Miss Casey."

"How are you doing, Eduardo?"

"Okay." He sounded subdued. "Jail is terrible."

"So I've heard. Listen, I saw Man Cave's show last night and met a couple of performers and RJ."

"You are helping me? Gracias, Miss Casey. You are angel from God."

"My friend wanted to see the show." No point in adding that her main goal was to protect Lily from Eduardo's legal trouble. "I saw a skinny guy in a suit and hat, maybe in his mid-twenties, talking with Danny in a dressing room. The guy acted like he owned the place. Any idea who he is?"

"He is Alden, Danny's drug supplier. Alden is also actor who writes plays for the stage."

"Oh." She wasn't sure what surprised her more, that Danny was buying drugs right on the premises or that Eduardo knew about it. "Steroids?"

"Cocaine, I think."

"Do the other dancers buy drugs, too?"

"I have not seen this. RJ hates employees to use

drugs. He caught Danny with a packet last month and they had big fight. RJ yelled if it happened again he would fire him, so I am surprised Alden was there. Danny must be desperate."

Was he that reckless or had he found leverage over RJ? "I wonder if that's created friction between the brothers." Casey told him about the shove Danny gave Randy as they left the stage. "I got the impression that Danny doesn't respect his brother very much."

"Danny does not respect anyone. Randy is afraid of him for good reason. Danny can be vicioso. Vicious." Eduardo wavered. "Danny whispers with Alden all the time. I think they have many secrets."

Interesting. "Have you by any chance overheard what they whisper about?"

"I heard them talk about cards, but that is all I can think of. My head is fuzzy ball right now." Eduardo cleared his throat. "I may remember things better after a shower and nap."

"Okay, and write down anything you recall. Bring it when you pick up your phone."

"I shall come this afternoon. I look forward to see-ing your be-eau-tiful face," Eduardo said.

Terrific. "Before you go, can you tell me about the other performers? We saw seven dancers and met the brothers, plus Hawaiian Brian."

"Brian is good guy. It is his sister who told him about the gold thong in Daphne's bed. The other four guys I do not know well. They only dance to pay for university and do not go to the parties."

"What parties?"

"Sometimes ladies pay us to perform at private parties. There was one last Sunday, but I was on my date with Daphne."

"Who else didn't go?"

"Danny and Randy do not go often. They are also stage actors who spend much time rehearsing and doing shows. You should talk to Brian about the others. He goes to every party. His number is in my phone."

"Thanks. See you later."

Casey sat on the bed and pondered what Eduardo had told her. Drugs. Secrets. Money and jealousy among competitive coworkers meant a lot was going on with the troupe. She'd witnessed the tension and some of their issues, which added credence to Eduardo's belief that he'd been framed. If it was true, then one of his coworkers wanted to destroy his life. Sure, Danny might be responsible, but what if the culprit was someone else?

Denver had faith in his colleague's ability to solve the case, but Casey wasn't as convinced. Given what some of the dancers had to hide, they wouldn't tell the cops much. Besides, the troupe was leaving town in two weeks and the cops already had their prime suspect in Eduardo, an uneducated visible minority who made his living taking off his clothes. Despite a witness's account of another man at Daphne Reynard's house that night, Eduardo's situation was still precarious. If a coworker thought Eduardo might walk away from this, he also could be in danger.

Also concerning was Lily's lack of response to her texts. Had something happened or was she deliberately avoiding her? Casey opened her laptop, looked up drivers' schedules, and confirmed that Lily's shift started at four this afternoon. With luck, her friend would be home this morning. Time for a face-to-face chat.

. . .

Lily lived in a single-story rancher on a small lot. On either side of the porch, hanging baskets of red and white begonias offered a vibrant contrast to the slate gray paint. Lily's Corolla wasn't around, but her husband Frank's grimy pickup was.

Frank emerged from the garage, pulling a lawnmower. A self-employed contractor, he turned down more jobs than he accepted, according to Lily. She said he preferred to work on his old car and get by on Lily's income. Frankie Junior trailed after him pushing a toy mower.

Casey thought about driving away, but Frank had seen her. On the occasions she'd come by for coffee, he hadn't been overly friendly. She needed to come up with a plausible story. Stepping out of the car, Casey could almost feel Frank's unwelcome stare trying to push her back.

"Casey." He gave a curt nod. "What brings you here?"

"I was hoping to speak to Lily about a work incident, but I don't see her car. Do you know when she'll be home?"

"No clue. She's running errands."

The longer Frank scrutinized her the deeper his scowl. "Did she send you here to spy on me?"

Casey gaped at him. "Why would Lily do that?"

"Whatever you two are scheming, it won't work."

What was he talking about? "There's no scheme, Frank, I promise." Casey kept her tone neutral, glancing at Frankie, who was pushing his mower around the yard. "I'm here because Lily witnessed an employee doing something he shouldn't have. It's a sensitive issue I didn't want to discuss at work." A good enough lie, she hoped.

"Then why not call her?"

"I left a couple of messages, but she hasn't called me back. I don't think Lily wants to be caught in the middle." The suspicion on Frank's face told her more questions were coming, things that might trip her up. "Look, I'll catch her later. Sorry to bother you."

Frank said nothing as Casey hurried back to her car. What was going on between those two? She slid behind the driver's wheel, chilled by Frank's persistent glare. Casey started the engine. Once away from the neighborhood, she pulled over and dialed Lily's number, but it went straight to voice mail.

"Lily, I dropped by your place to see you and wound up talking with Frank. He believes you and I are spying on him. I didn't ask why, but I think I've created a problem. Anyway, I told him I needed to discuss a sensitive work incident with you, so call me, okay? It's almost noon and I'm heading to MPT now."

# SEVEN

Casey pulled into MPT's parking lot as Marie stepped out of her SUV. Sporting sunglasses, shorts, and a baggy T-shirt, she schlepped toward the entrance in flip-flops.

Grinning, Casey jogged up to her. "Aloha, Marie! Didn't expect to see you this morning."

Marie stopped and turned around. "Timesheet's due and I have to finish an incident report I was supposed to hand in yesterday. Why are you here?"

"Tons of paperwork."

Marie could have completed her timesheet and report at home. Had her kids been giving her a hard time about the hangover?

"You look pale." Casey followed her into the admin building, noting that Marie kept the shades on. "Maybe you need a Hawaiian vacation."

Marie spun around. "Zip it!"

She grinned. "So, you remember last night."

"It was a dumb mistake, that's all. Not worth talking about."

"Okay, but just one question. Did you hear Brian or anyone mention drugs or the name Eduardo?"

Marie huffed. "I was a little preoccupied, Casey."

"*Preoccupied?*" Casey smirked. "Is that your Scrabble word for horny?"

"Stop!" She raised her palm. "You and I will never speak of this again, understand?"

"Come on, Marie, how would you react if I were in your shoes?"

Marie glanced around the parking lot. "Whatever." Her shoulders slumped. "By the way, I lost one of my earrings last night. It's a gold hoop about the size of a dime. Don't suppose you found it in your car?"

"No, but I'll have a look."

"Thanks. It's only gold-plated, but the earrings were a birthday present from the kids."

"If it's not in my car, it could be between the dumpsters in the alley or inside the venue."

"Oh, hell."

"I might have to go back there 'cause I need to talk to your Hawaiian. Got a coconut bra you can dust off in case you want another tour?"

Marie whipped off her sunglasses. "Keep pushing it and I won't give you something useful."

"Such as?"

"Promise you won't blab about what happened last night?"

"I have no intention of telling staff, although Lou knows."

"At least he's not a gossip." Marie removed a business card from her handbag. "I found this in my bra when I got home. I have no idea how it got there." She shuddered. "I mean, it's like his ginormous hands were everywhere at once."

Casey read the name Brian Kalolo, along with an email and phone number. She didn't look forward to talking with the sleazeball. For all she knew, Hawaiian Brian could be part of a conspiracy to frame Eduardo, given that he wanted to be a headliner. No one connected to Man Cave could be ruled out, especially not Alden, or even RJ. Who knew what Eduardo might have inadvertently seen, heard, or done to threaten their interests? Casey dropped the card in her purse.

"What do you want to talk to Brian about?" Marie asked. "Not me, I hope."

"No, and you probably don't want to involve yourself in his business."

"Damn right." Marie trudged to the women's locker room.

Casey headed upstairs to the security department and immersed herself in paperwork until Stan appeared.

"Okay, you two, I need your timesheets within the hour." He turned to Marie. "What happened to you?"

Slouched in her chair, Marie slurped her coffee.

"Late night," she mumbled.

"Uh-huh." He turned back to Casey. "What did you end up doing with the suspect's phone?"

"I took it to lost-and-found." Casey handed Stan her timesheet. "Eduardo's been released and is picking it up later today."

Stan peered at her. "You won't discuss the murder with him, will you?"

"What's this about a murder?" Marie perked up. "And who's Eduardo?"

Great. The biggest blabbermouth at MPT wanted the scoop, and she wouldn't let this go until she had answers. Casey's look-what-you've-done stare at Stan sent him scurrying to his office. She turned and updated Marie, leaving out any reference to Lily.

"So, that's why we went to the show. You were on a fact-finding mission, and now you want to talk to the Hawaiian." Marie's face grew pale. "Wait. Is he a suspect?"

"Maybe."

Marie bent over and smacked her forehead on the desk. "I hate my life."

. . .

Casey stood up and stretched, her tasks finally completed. Normally, she'd be on her way home but she wanted to talk to Lily, who was still ignoring her texts.

It was nearly three o'clock. Lily usually arrived for work early, so she'd probably be here soon. Casey headed downstairs to the lunchroom, fetched a can of pop from the machine, and chatted with a couple of drivers. Minutes later, she wandered into the women's locker room. No Lily. Might as well spend the time searching for Marie's earring while waiting for Lily.

When she reached her old Tercel, Casey rolled down the driver's window and left the doors open to get rid of the stifling summer heat. Scouring the backseat, floor mats, and everything in between, she had no luck. The earring was either in the alley or in the venue.

Lily pulled into the parking lot. Head down, she strolled toward the entrance.

"Lily?" Casey called out.

Lily spun around, her mouth twisted in a grimace. "You shouldn't have come to my home."

"I'm sorry," Casey replied. "I honestly didn't think a visit would cause any harm. Why does Frank think I'm spying on him?"

Lily fidgeted. "Long story."

"Can we talk in my car? It'll give us some privacy." Lily looked like she wanted to bolt, which worried Casey. "Eduardo's lawyer probably knows about the text sent from your phone. He'll want to talk to you. The cops might drop by, too." She didn't have the heart to add that Denver Davies also knew. "Let's sort this out before it comes to that, okay?"

Lily let out a soft moan. "What am I going to do?"

"If I know what's going on, maybe I can help you figure it out." Casey halted. "See, I think you were telling the truth about not sending the text to Eduardo. So, I have to ask, did someone else use your phone that night?" Lily's ripening cheeks told her the answer.

"Let's go to your car," Lily mumbled.

They didn't speak until they'd settled in. Lily slunk down in the passenger's seat.

"Eduardo's out on bail," Casey said.

"That's good, I guess."

Casey's eyebrows rose. "I thought you'd be happier, or at least more relieved."

"With all that's going on, maybe it was a mistake to befriend him." She picked at a cuticle. "A dumb way to get back at Frank."

Casey's eyebrows rose. "I don't understand."

Lily exhaled slowly. "Frank's been cheating on me."

"Oh, Lily."

Lily gazed out the side window. "I confronted him a few weeks ago and, naturally, he denied everything. Now Frank's terrified I'll find proof. It's why he's paranoid about being watched." She turned to Casey. "The loser doesn't know that the private investigator I hired has already shown me photos and videos of him with other women. My lawyer says I have a strong case for getting full custody of Frankie."

"Ah. This is why you've been so worried about consequences if the cops show up at your door, and why Frank thinks you've been spying on him."

Lily nodded. "If he finds out that Eduardo and I have been meeting for coffee a couple of times a week, my leverage could disappear."

"I understand that part, but what I don't get is who used your phone Sunday night?"

Lily slouched further down the seat and closed her eyes. "This is so embarrassing."

"I'm not judging, I just need to know."

Opening her eyes, she turned to Casey. "I met a guy named Marcos on my bus three weeks ago. We had coffee a couple of times, nothing else."

Casey's stomach sank. She knew Lily was lonely, but to indulge in late-night coffee dates with men she barely knew was risky.

"Did you meet at the same diner you and Eduardo went to?"

"It's the only all-night place on my route."

"What's his last name?"

"Didn't ask. Didn't think it mattered." She glanced at Casey. "Guess I have a thing for hot Latinos."

"They are pretty hard to resist."

But even for multicultural Vancouver, two sexy men on Lily's bus route at night was no coincidence. In Man Cave's brochure, Eduardo was the only Latino and none of the crew were named Marcos. Still, half of the guys used stage names. With spray tans, body makeup, and wigs, some of them could resemble Eduardo's ethnicity, she supposed.

"What did Marcos look like?" Casey asked.

"Lighter skin than Eduardo. Muscular body. Shoulder-length, dark brown hair with blond streaks. He dressed well and wore a diamond-studded watch."

Not a match for any of the dancers Casey had seen.

"What do you know about him?"

"Only that DUIs kept him from driving, or so he said." She wrinkled her nose. "Turns out the guy was a jerk."

Casey leaned closer. "How so?"

Lily took a deep breath. "Marcos called the night of the murder and said he needed to see me right away."

"When, exactly, did he call?"

"Just after ten. He said his father had a stroke and he'd be on a flight to Mexico early the next morning." Lily paused. "I wasn't feeling up for a coffee date, but he insisted. Said he had a special gift for me and asked if I could meet with him between eleven and eleven-thirty. Like an idiot, I gave in. Got there just before eleven-thirty and told him I had only a five-minute break."

"Did you happen to ask if Marcos and Eduardo knew one another?"

"I did, 'cause Marcos reminded me of Eduardo. He told me he'd never heard of him."

A total lie. "So, Marcos used your phone?"

Lily fiddled with the strap on her handbag. "I had to use the bathroom, and he asked to borrow it while I was gone 'cause his battery had died. When I came back, Marcos and my phone had vanished. He left a note on a napkin, saying another emergency had come up and that he'd return the phone around one-thirty. I was so pissed off. My shift ended at one, so I had to get back to MPT, pick up my car, then drive back to the bloody diner. I got there at one-thirty, intending to give Marcos shit, but he'd already taken off and left the phone with the server."

So, Lily had missed running into Eduardo by a half hour.

"Is that when you saw the text and learned that Eduardo had been trying to get in touch with you?"

"Yeah."

"Why didn't you tell Eduardo about Marcos?"

"Like I said, I was embarrassed and didn't know what was going on." Lily blew out a puff of air. "Clearly, there was something weird between those two and I didn't want to get in the middle of it."

"Which is where I came in," Casey said.

Lily nodded. "All I wanted was for Eduardo to stop asking me about the stupid text and let it go. Then you told me about the murder, which made me wonder if Marcos was somehow involved."

"I understand how you felt, Lily. Still, I wish you'd told me earlier."

"I know," she murmured. "It's just that I was afraid

you'd think I was pathetic."

"You're not, Lily, and don't ever think that."

Lily fiddled with her purse strap. "Anyway, Marcos disappeared and deleted his number from my contact list. The only evidence I have of his existence is the silver bracelet he gave me."

"Marcos actually came through with a gift?"

"Yeah. Guess he was afraid I'd turn around and leave if he didn't produce something." She rubbed her cheek. "How could I turn down his request to borrow my phone when he'd given me a present?"

"Do you still have the bracelet?"

"In my locker, and feel free to take the damn thing. I don't need a reminder about my stupidity. Maybe you'll find fingerprints or something." Lily straightened up, fear animating her face. "Marcos has to wonder if the cops would learn about all this. What if he's worried about evidence that could implicate him and wants the bracelet back?" She gripped Casey's arm. "Marcos knows where I work!"

"Lily, stay calm. I'll have Stan arrange for one of us to ride with you." An idea struck Casey but vanished the moment a familiar pickup truck roared into the lot.

"Damn," Lily muttered. "It's Frank."

# EIGHT

"**Y**ou don't have to talk to him," Casey said.

"I'm not afraid." Lily flung the door open. "Might as well get this over with."

Frank jumped out of the truck. "What the hell are you up to, Lily?"

"Where's Frankie?"

"Next door with Janet."

"Bloody wonderful." Lily plunked her hands on her hips. "You shouldn't have come here."

"You won't talk to me at home, so what am I supposed to do?"

"You wanna talk? Fine." She marched toward him. "I know you've been cheating on me, you bastard."

Frank gawked at Lily, his mouth falling open.

Uh-oh. Casey got out of the car and edged closer until Frank spotted her.

"You!" He stepped forward and pointed at Casey. "This is your fault, coming to my house and stirring things up."

Great, he wanted a scapegoat. Casey didn't respond.

"This isn't about Casey," Lily shot back. "It's about me filing for divorce."

Frank recoiled as if he'd been slapped in the face.

"No! Lily, come on. That's crazy."

"I know about Janet and Beth-Ann. Screwing my friends was cruel and stupid, Frank."

Her friends? Casey cringed.

Two mechanics strolling through the parking lot stopped, then meandered up to Casey.

"Everything okay?" one of them murmured.

"Not really. If you've got a minute, can you stay?"

"No problem."

"I was right," Frank yelled. "You had Casey spy on me."

"Wrong, you idiot! Beth-Ann gave herself away at the hair salon. She took one look at me and turned beet red. Couldn't even talk, which only confirmed what I already knew."

Frank's mouth was opening and closing like a fish gasping for air.

"I saw the looks you've been giving each other since Easter, and I overheard the phone calls. So, I hired a PI." Lily glared at Frank. "He's got photos and videos, Frank."

"So what? That shit can be faked."

Lily rolled her eyes.

Lou eased the bus into the yard, his shift over. Excellent timing, Casey thought. The extra backup might be needed.

"Beth-Ann was in our bed Saturday night." Lily's voice quivered. "Frankie got up to pee and saw her coming out of the bathroom, naked." She choked back a sob. "When I got home, you were snoring your ass off and our son was sleeping on the floor in his closet.

He was scared and confused, you moron."

Casey inhaled sharply. Poor little guy.

The color drained from Frank's face. "Look, I'm sorry. I've been stressed and made big mistakes, but we can go to counseling or something. It won't happen again, I swear. We can work this out, right? I love you, Lily."

Casey crossed her arms. Typical dumb-ass response. Her first husband, Greg, tried the same tactic fifteen years ago.

"Not interested. You and I are so done." Lily wiped her eyes. "Go home, pack your stuff, and get out of my house."

"No. way." Frank shook his head. "It's *our* house, Lily. You can't make me go."

"My brothers will. They're heading there now."

"Wait!" Frank's forehead glistened. "Please, Lily, we've been through too much together. We've built a life."

"A lousy one, Frank, and it's over now."

Frank scratched the back of his neck. "It's not all my fault, you know. I was alone every damn weekend. You didn't even try to change your shifts."

"Because you were supposed to be working, so I needed to be home for Frankie during the day."

"You didn't care what I wanted."

"Well, I sure as hell don't now. Take off, Frank. You're on private property."

Lou joined Casey as Marie emerged from the admin building. Everyone stared at Frank, who was clenching his fists and scowling at Lily.

"I'll have my sister pick up Frankie and he can stay

with her tonight," Lily said. "If you're still in our house when I get home, I'll call your father."

Casey exchanged a puzzled look with Lou. A weird threat, yet the ferocity disappeared from Frank's face. The jerk mumbled something, then climbed into his truck and peeled out of the lot. Lily started to cry.

Marie hurried up to her and put her arm around her. Casey handed Lily a tissue.

When Lily calmed down, Casey said, "Will Frank give you more grief?"

"No, I've got enough leverage to keep him in line."

"He looked furious," Marie said. "Are you sure you'll be safe?"

"Yeah, I'll be okay. Frank yells a lot but he's not violent. My sister invited me to stay with her a while anyway, so I might do that."

"Does the leverage have something to do with his dad?" Casey asked.

Lily nodded. "My father-in-law's a self-made millionaire with a strong moral compass. He'd already threatened to cut Frank out of his will if he didn't start working harder. The affairs and our divorce'll seal his fate."

"Come with me," Marie said. "Let's grab a coffee."

The two women went inside while Casey hung back with Lou. Lily's domestic worries might not be over. If Frank or her father-in-law found out about her coffee dates with other men, she could lose full custody of Frankie. The loss would crush her.

# NINE

One of the dispatchers peeked into the lunchroom, spotted Casey, then gestured to someone in the hallway. Moments later, Eduardo appeared.

"Hola, Miss Casey!" Beaming at her, he strutted toward the table she shared with Lou and Marie.

Marie plunked her coffee mug down. "Holy moly! My dream guy just arrived."

Employees in the room gawked at him, the women with admiration, the men in disbelief. Eduardo barely noticed as he kept his gaze on Casey. She had to admit he looked spectacular in the aviator sunglasses, black jeans, and chest-hugging white T-shirt.

"Let me guess," Lou remarked. "The stripper you told me about?"

"Yep."

"What?" Marie sat up straighter. "He wasn't dancing last night."

"Remember the matador in Man Cave's brochure?"

Marie squinted at Eduardo until her face lit up.

"That's Don Juan Dong!"

Pepsi spurted from Lou's mouth. "Seriously?" He wiped up the mess.

"Cool stage name, huh?" Casey chuckled and patted

Lou's back. "How ya doing, Eduardo?"

"*This* is Eduardo?" Marie's eyebrows arched so high they disappeared under her bangs.

"The one and only." She introduced everybody.

Eduardo bowed to Marie. "I am enchanted." He turned to Lou. "And you." He pointed at him. "You are lucky hombre. Your wife is be-eau-tiful and smart and brave."

"That she is." Lou winked at her.

Eduardo scrutinized Lou from head to toe. "You have good face and body. Can you dance? You would make much money."

"We could use the extra income." Casey smirked. "And I'm sure plenty of customers would love to stuff your thong. We'd have to give you a cool stage name, though."

"I could come up with a few," Marie remarked, then sipped her coffee.

Lou didn't blush often, but even his freckles were turning a dark plum.

"All you must do is buff up more." Eduardo removed his jacket and flexed his enormous biceps. "Is good, no?"

"Is fabulous." Marie licked her lips, then turned to Lou. "You'll need a spray tan and baby oil, too."

Casey snickered. "I'm sure Eduardo could teach you to gyrate your hips to music."

"The música is fantástico." Closing his eyes, Eduardo dipped and swayed his shoulders while snapping his fingers. Marie applauded.

"One job's more than enough, thanks." Lou pushed

his chair back. "Time to get some takeout. Pizza okay, Casey?"

"Sure. I'll be home by four-thirty."

He nodded and charged out of the room.

"That was awesome." Marie chuckled, then turned to Eduardo. "So, how did you meet our Miss Casey?"

"Remember the harassment complaints about a guy who wanted to paint women's portraits?" She nodded toward Eduardo.

"No!" Marie gaped at him. "Why would anyone complain about you?"

"I ask this too." The corners of Eduardo's mouth drooped. "Is perplexing beyond belief."

"Well, sweetheart, you can paint my portrait anytime," Marie said.

Eduardo again bowed. "It would be great honor."

"When's your next performance?" Marie asked. "I'd love to see you dance."

"Tonight."

His answer surprised Casey. Wouldn't it be safer if he waited until the cops caught the killer?

"Tell me," Marie said, "how'd you wind up charged with murder?"

"Is tragic story."

Eduardo pulled out an orange plastic chair and was about to sit down when Lily entered the room. Now in uniform, she headed for the coffee machine.

"Lily!" Eduardo rushed toward her.

Lily tossed an uneasy glance around the room. Understandable, Casey thought. Eduardo's interest in her would trigger plenty of gossip.

"They seem to know each other," Marie said. "So,

how friendly are they?"

"They chat when things are quiet on Lily's route, and don't let anyone think otherwise, okay?" Casey warned. "She's got enough to deal with. You know how stressful divorce is."

Marie's expression softened. "Three bloody times."

After Lily hurried out of the room, Eduardo returned to Casey and Marie, his smile gone.

"Lily said you know who sent me that text, Miss Casey, "but she would not say more."

"What text?" Marie asked. "What's going on?"

"This isn't a good time to get into it," Casey answered. "I need a private word with Eduardo, if you don't mind. It's kind of urgent."

Marie sat back in her chair. "More secrets?"

"It's about respecting Eduardo's privacy." She returned Marie's challenging glare. "After last night, surely you can appreciate the need for discretion."

Marie gathered her things. "Nice meeting you, Eduardo."

"Is pleasure to meet you as well."

Watching her leave the room, Casey said, "Did you get your phone, Eduardo?"

"No, I come to see you first."

Casey slid her chair back. "Our lost-and-found clerk's going to love you."

The clerk, Angie, dropped her clipboard as Eduardo ambled toward her. After Casey made the introductions, Angie dabbed the corners of her mouth with a tissue. Good grief, was the woman salivating?

"The phone I turned in belongs to him," Casey told

her.

"Got it right here."

Angie bent down and removed a plastic bin from beneath the counter. When she handed Eduardo his phone, her fingertips grazed his hand.

"Gracias, señorita."

"De nada, el amigo."

"Ah! You speak Spanish?"

"Un poco."

"Your hair is so bright with the blues and greens, like a peacock. And the nose ring! I am loving that."

Angie's giggles were overshadowed by the laughter of two women behind them, watching the interaction. Casey didn't know them well. Both were new drivers.

"We should get going." She escorted Eduardo outside. "Were you able to recall anything from those whispered chats between Danny and Alden?"

Eduardo removed a folded scrap of paper from his back pocket and handed it to her.

Casey read the number 35,000 and the first names of three women. "That's all?"

Eduardo spotted the drivers, who'd followed them.

"Hola, be-eau-tiful ladies!"

"Hola yourself, handsome!" one of them replied, her eyes raking him over while she continued toward the buses.

"Eduardo!" Casey turned him in another direction. "Can you focus, please?"

"My mother and sisters taught me to be kind to all ladies, Miss Casey."

"Did she also teach you that there's a time and place for everything?"

He put on his sunglasses. "There is always time for ladies."

Casey rubbed her chin as she assessed him. "Eduardo, you seem like a decent guy, but are you aware that your accent and obsession with women is kind of an overdone cliché? The way you speak could mean that people won't take you seriously."

Eduardo looked around the parking lot, then stepped closer until he was only inches from her face.

"I was hired for my ethnicity, Casey. RJ said Man Cave's fans expect the stereotype, so I give them what they want." His accent and awkward phrases were gone. "The man knew what he was talking about. The tips are amazing."

Casey smiled. "There you are."

He stepped back and gave her a deep bow.

"Do your coworkers know?" she asked.

"Only RJ. The others think I'm a stupid foreigner with more fans and money than I deserve." Eduardo scratched the back of his neck. "Truth is, the money's too good to walk away from."

"Does Lily know?" she asked.

Eduardo smiled. "She prefers the accent. It's fun, harmless escapism, and she needs that." His smile faded. "Though I doubt she wants anything from me right now."

True enough. "What else about you isn't quite real, Eduardo?"

"Nothing. Like I said when we met, I really am looking for love, and I love to paint, and I am from Ecuador," he answered. "My mother risked her life to get us to Canada, then worked her butt off to put food on the table and pay the rent. I started working at sixteen to help out and still do. I owe Mom everything. There was a lot of violence where we lived. Gangs. Drugs. I probably would have died."

"I can believe it."

"Speaking of death, there's something you should know." Eduardo's expression grew solemn. "Danny took Daphne to dinner one night, and she told me it didn't go well."

"What happened?"

"Daphne wanted to pay for her meal and left her credit card on the table while she went to the washroom. When she stopped to answer her phone, she turned and saw Danny snapping pictures of her card. She canceled it the next day." He blinked at Casey. "He's the scammer, isn't he?"

"Sounds like it." Casey studied the names on the sheet of paper. "And these three women could be his victims. Danny would have had to use his own name with Daphne because she knew who he was from the show." She tapped the paper. "But if these women didn't know you, Danny could have used your name to implicate you in the scam. Those cards you overheard him and Alden discussing were probably credit cards, which means Alden's in on the scheme."

"Makes sense. Alden's more than Danny's drug dealer. They're good friends who apparently met while performing in the same play." Eduardo took a gulp of air. "I think one of them killed Daphne."

"It's possible. If either of them tried to use her card number the next day and found it already canceled, they'd know she hadn't trusted Danny."

"He'd be pissed." Eduardo leaned against a sedan. "Danny has a temper."

Now that Eduardo was out of jail and sharing his side of the story, Danny might want to shut him up. Was his phone still being tracked? Casey glanced around MPT's half-full parking lot. Heatwaves rose from the asphalt on this sweltering day. She studied the vehicles parked on the street. Beyond MPT's chain-link fence bordering the sidewalk, few people were out.

"Eduardo, have you ever heard of a man named Marcos? His body type's similar to yours and he rides Lily's bus."

"No, why?"

"He used Lily's phone to send you that text Sunday night."

"What the hell for?"

"The guy wanted you out of Daphne's house so he, or an accomplice, could kill her. It was also a way to ensure you wouldn't have an alibi."

"Why would a stranger do that?"

"I doubt he's a stranger."

Eduardo adjusted his sunglasses. "Who then?"

Before Frank had roared into the parking lot, Casey was about to run an idea past Lily. All the drama had pushed it out of her thoughts until this moment. Casey checked her watch. Lily's shift had started. She removed the Man Cave brochure from her bag and opened it.

"Hold this up, will you? I want to take a photo."

She snapped a photo and sent it to Lily with a text. *Are any of these guys Marcos?*

Casey said, "I think someone's been tracking your movements through your phone. Your calendar and texts reveal a lot about your activities."

Eduardo spotted several employees strolling out of the admin building toward staff parking.

One of the women pointed at him and said, "That's the hot guy I saw in the lunchroom."

"Showtime." Eduardo cleared his throat. "I do not use phone tracking app, Miss Casey."

Now that she'd heard his normal voice, the heavy accent was even less appealing. "Eduardo, there are other ways to follow someone. I live with a teenager who kept so many secrets that I started researching tracking apps a while back. Long story short, I didn't track her phone, but I learned enough to know how sneaky and undetectable tracking can be."

"You are a mamá?" His face lit up. "Excelente! Is great blessing."

"Legal guardian, actually, and yeah, things are good right now."

It thrilled Casey that Summer had become involved with environmental causes. She was happy and looking forward to her sixteenth birthday in a couple of weeks. Casey's phone pinged.

Lily's text read, *Samurai Danny is Marcos but different hair and skin tone!*

Of course. As a performer, Danny had access to makeup and costumes and had probably practiced different accents. Casey texted back, *Thanks!*

"Lily just confirmed that Danny and Marcos are the

same person."

"Bastard!" Eduardo began pacing.

Casey again looked up and down the street. A red Jeep cruised by, but she couldn't see the driver from here. The idea that someone might be watching them made her edgy. At least employees were around, heading to and from the admin building.

"What kind of car does Danny drive?"

"Is metallic gray Jaguar. Why do you ask this?"

"Just curious. Do you know what Alden drives, by any chance?"

"No."

Casey mulled over Eduardo's information. "Listen, I don't think you should perform tonight. It's not a good idea to be anywhere near Danny or Alden."

"But I have already lost much money." He ran his hand through his hair. "I should talk to RJ and Brian. They see and hear many things, maybe something that could solve these crimes."

Casey doubted it. "It's too risky, Eduardo. Danny won't want you returning to work and things could get nasty."

Sweat appeared on his brow. "Will you speak to RJ and Brian for me?"

"I'm guessing the police have already talked to them or soon will."

"RJ does not trust la policía." Eduardo glanced at a driver walking by. "Is why he does not tell them about Alden's drug deals."

"Is there a reason he doesn't trust them?"

"I heard he has had many traffic tickets, but maybe

there are other things I do not know."

"Your lawyer should hire a private investigator to find out everything that's going on with Man Cave and their associates."

Eduardo shook his head. "I cannot afford this. Please, Miss Casey, talk to RJ and Brian."

The thought of a face-to-face chat with either of them bothered her. "Can't you call them? You've got to call in sick anyway."

"RJ will be so mad if I do not dance tonight that he will not want to answer questions. Is better if you talk to him and Brian in person."

"Are you sure you can trust Brian to be honest with me?"

"Si, he is good friend. When his sister asked if any of the performers wore a gold thong, he said he did not know, which was not true. Brian knows I would never harm Daphne."

"So, I'm guessing he didn't tell his sister about you and Daphne?"

"No." Eduardo clasped her hands. "I beg for your help, Miss Casey."

Casey again surveyed the parking lot and street. Man Cave was leaving town soon. Danny might want to clear up whatever loose ends were left. She looked around once more and texted Lily: *If Marcos shows up, hit the panic button. Don't take a break at the diner. A guard will join you before dark. I'll explain later.*

Seconds later, Lily texted back with surprised and thumbs-up emojis.

Perhaps Brian and RJ were the most direct way to gather useful info for the cops. Since she hadn't found

Marie's earring, she had an excuse to go back there.

"What time do RJ and Brian arrive for work?"

"RJ shows up by six, Brian is there by six-thirty. He takes long time to oil the body."

"I bet," she replied. "Listen, if you promise not to go to work tonight, I'll talk to them. Maybe you have a lady who needs escorting somewhere?"

Eduardo pondered this, then snapped his fingers.

"Si! I was invited to big charity event but had to decline for work."

"Call her. And keep your eyes open when heading home, especially if no one else is around. And don't tell Brian I'm heading there. The less he knows the safer he is."

"Gracias, Miss Casey. You are special friend. Bring your husband to the show. He will learn good dance moves. I must leave you and call my lady friend."

"Stay safe." After Eduardo left, she called Kendal. "I've got to talk to Man Cave's manager and Hawaiian Brian tonight. Want to come along?"

"Only if you don't bring that maniac Marie."

"I won't."

"Then I'm in."

"The plan is to approach them in the parking lot when they arrive, so we might not need to go inside. Can you be ready in about ninety minutes?"

"Sure, but Randy's already left a message, asking to cash in on the rain check."

"A chat with him could be useful, but don't call Randy back yet till we decide for sure." Casey watched a Dodge Caravan drive by.

"Why, what's going on?"

"I'll fill you in when I see you."

Casey hoped she wasn't putting Kendal in danger. Randy might not like Danny, but they were still brothers. How far would Randy go to protect him?

# TEN

Casey gripped her purse as Kendal floored the BMW.

"Feel free to slow down, girlfriend. We're not that late."

"You want to get there before RJ shows up, right?"

True. Casey would have preferred to drive, but since they planned to approach RJ and Hawaiian Brian in the parking lot, Kendal's car would make a better impression than her old Tercel. On the way, Casey shared her theory about Danny's involvement in fraud and murder, and Alden's possible role in the crimes.

"What about our favorite handyman, Randy?" Kendal asked. "Think he's part of this?"

"I've been wondering about it," Casey replied. "We also need to consider that Danny killed Daphne on his own. I know where the diner is and there would have been little traffic at that time of night. He could have gone from there to Daphne's in fifteen minutes or less and showed up just as Eduardo was leaving."

"I feel bad for your friend Lily," Kendal replied. "Who knew that a few coffee dates would result in such a mess?"

No kidding. Stan had left several messages on Lily's

phone, asking her to call him, but she hadn't. Concerned for Lily's safety, Casey told him everything that was going on with her. It prompted Stan to assign one of their toughest security officers to join Lily tonight. Stan also agreed not to say anything to Lily's supervisors, for now. In exchange, he expected to be kept in the loop.

"I spoke with Denver Davies after I called you," Casey told Kendal. "Since Eduardo's release from jail, Daphne's credit cards have been compromised. The killer must have taken her cards and is trying to turn the cops' focus back on Eduardo."

"Not good. Eduardo could be picked up anytime, which I assume is Danny and Alden's plan."

"Looks that way."

Denver had put her in touch with Detective Bojaski, one of the homicide investigators. She repeated what Eduardo had said about Danny and Alden's drug deals, plus a possible connection between them, the credit card scams, and Daphne's murder. Bojaski wasn't impressed until she mentioned the text from Lily's phone and the gift from Marcos. She should have realized that physical evidence would pique his interest, at least a little. Since she didn't have time to bring the silver bracelet to him, she'd agreed to seal it in a plastic bag and leave it with MPT's dispatch center, where an officer would pick it up.

Kendal pulled into the parking lot next to the old warehouse, half of which had been converted into the two-hundred-seat entertainment venue. The location in historic Gastown likely attracted both locals and tourists who enjoyed the pubs, shops, and galleries in one of Vancouver's oldest and once infamous neighborhoods. The parking lot itself had seen better days. Kendal slowly navigated around potholes and over crumbling asphalt.

"Don't park too close to the building," Casey said. "I don't want us to be spotted."

"It's not a big lot, Casey."

Kendal cruised to the farthest corner, then backed into a stall beside a wooden fence. Through the holes in the old fence, Casey saw rail tracks and beyond that Vancouver Harbour. She also noticed the entrance to the alley behind the warehouse.

Five minutes later, a white Ford Escalade pulled in and parked near the building. Brian stepped out, wearing shorts and a muscle shirt.

"Aloha," Kendal murmured. "Let's talk to the horn dog."

She stepped out of the car, called his name, and waved. Brian flashed a broad smile, then sauntered toward them, ogling Kendal's tight black dress.

"You gals are early," he said. "Doors aren't open yet."

*Gals?* Casey cringed.

"We're going for dinner first," Kendal replied.

Brian looked beyond Kendal and Casey. "Your friend not with you?"

Casey shook her head. "Not this time."

His gaze lingered over Kendal's cleavage. "Well, you're here. Even better."

Casey smirked at Kendal, whose smile was frozen in place.

"I'm a friend of Eduardo's," Casey began, "and he said you might help me with information."

Brian's mouth twitched. "About what?"

"He told me that you and the troupe were invited to a party last Sunday night. I was wondering if Randy and Danny were there?"

He scratched his jaw. "You want to know if they have alibis for that woman's murder?"

The guy was sharper than she thought. "That's why Eduardo asked me to talk to you. He was hoping you might have seen or heard something."

"You think he's innocent?" Brian asked.

"I do."

"Me too." He shifted his feet. "It's so damn disturbing to think someone I work with is responsible for Mrs. Reynard's death. She was real nice."

Why wasn't he answering her question? "About the party?"

"Right." Brian glanced around as if worried about being overheard. "All the guys were there, except Eduardo and Danny, but Danny often has his own gigs and other stuff going on. I have no idea when Randy left."

"Would that other stuff have anything to do with a drug dealer named Alden?" Kendal asked.

"I meant acting jobs." Brian again looked up and down the alley. "Alden's bad news."

"So we've heard," Casey remarked. "Is Randy into drugs too?"

"Just booze. He hates Danny's coke habit. Anyway, that's about all I know. No one's talking much these days. The murder and Eduardo's arrest have made everyone uptight."

A Porsche pulled into the lot.

"That's RJ," Brain said. "Gotta go." He kissed Kendal's hand. "I'll do something extra special for you."

"Can't wait."

"By the way, I don't suppose you found my friend's gold-hoop earring?" Casey asked. "She's pretty sure she lost it either inside the building or in the alley."

"Sorry, no." Brian winked at Kendal. "See ya later, gorgeous."

As he hurried off, Kendal wiped her hand with a tissue. "I don't want to think about where his hand has been."

"Speaking of unsavory places, and I apologize for asking," Casey said, "but could you look for Marie's earring between the dumpsters while I'll talk to RJ?"

"This is not the fun time I anticipated," Kendal grumbled. "You owe me."

"I'll buy the first round."

"Two rounds."

While Kendal headed for the dumpsters, Casey caught up with RJ at the back door.

"Excuse me, RJ?" Casey said. "We met last night. I'm Casey, a friend of Eduardo's."

He looked from her to Kendal, who was scouring the ground with her phone's flashlight. Even from here, Casey smelled the decaying food and tried not to crinkle her nose.

"What's she doing?" he asked.

"Looking for our friend's missing earring."

Casey launched into her reason for coming here and

brought up Alden's drug deals on the premises. She hoped that mentioning his name would gain more co-operation than accusing one of his employees of a crime.

RJ stared at her. "You're not a cop, are you?"

"No, I work in security with Mainland Public Transport. I met Eduardo on one of our buses. He's a good guy and we're trying to help him." More cars pulled into the lot. "If we don't figure this out soon, the police will show up here."

"Some cop already left a voice mail." RJ pointed his finger at her. "What makes you think you can solve this?"

"I've assisted the police a few times."

"I don't want you questioning my employees."

Casey's patience withered. "Fine, but can you at least tell me Alden's last name, so I can do a little more digging on him?"

"If you can help bust that freak, it'd make my day." RJ removed his phone from an inside jacket pocket. "I don't know his last name, but I got his license plate number in case I needed to call the cops."

Casey snapped a photo of his screen. She'd barely finished before RJ stepped inside and shut the door.

Kendal joined her. "No luck with the earring. Learn anything from the manager?"

"Alden's license plate number. Let's head back to the car. I brought my laptop."

"Clever girl," Kendal said. "I still think you should apply to the Vancouver Police Department. It'd be so cool to train together. You'd make a brilliant detective."

"Thanks."

Casey hadn't decided if she was ready for a career change, especially when she tended to break a law occasionally, like she was about to. She removed her laptop from the car's backseat, slid into the front, and got to work.

"Are you hacking into a database?" Kendal leaned close to her. "Where'd you learn that?"

"From a friend."

"Anyone I know? Because I find that an attractive quality in a man."

"He doesn't like people much." She peered at the screen. "Only tolerates me because I helped him write a couple of papers in a criminology class. The guy's brilliant with computers but can barely write a complete sentence." Casey sat back. "Damn. Alden drives a Cadillac registered to Sadie Edenshaw Fowler who lives in Prince George. Not reported stolen."

"Meaning it likely belongs to a girlfriend or relative over three hundred miles away."

"Maybe." Casey kept searching, but nothing came up. "There's no driver's license listed under any combination of surnames. I'll google him." After a few more keystrokes, she said, "Nothing on social media. It's like the man doesn't exist."

"He's using a fake identity. Big surprise," Kendal remarked. "Maybe Randy, or this Sadie woman, can tell us something."

"No, a friend or relative might alert him."

"Or hate Alden and want him in jail," Kendal replied. "Randy might know more about the guy."

A metallic gray Jaguar pulled into the lot and parked near the entrance.

"That's Danny! Duck!" Casey scrunched down, then raised her head just enough to see him step out of the vehicle and head for the door. "He's gone inside."

Randy drove up in a shiny red Corvette. When he stepped out, Casey noticed the light gray dress pants and white short-sleeved shirt. Definitely more dressed up than his brother. Had Randy made plans for after the show?

Kendal opened the car door. "Another chance for info."

"Don't mention Danny." Casey's stomach clenched. "We have no idea if Randy can be trusted. Maybe we should wait and talk about how to approach him."

"Let me just ask if he's available after the show."

"Are you sure that's a good idea?"

"Yep."

They both stepped out of the car.

"Be careful," Casey said. Although Kendal was more than capable of handling herself, guys like Randy were equally adept at reading them.

Kendal sashayed toward him. "Hi, Randy!"

The surprise on his face turned to admiration as he checked Kendal out.

"Great to see you again," Randy said. "Can I cash in on that rain check after the show?"

"Totally," Kendal replied. "I thought it best to arrange something in person, which is partly why we came early."

"Awesome." He turned to Casey and smiled. "Hey, there. I'm glad you're back."

"Thanks. We were hoping to talk with you."

"Same here." He sighed as if relieved. "Danny and I share a condo in Coal Harbour. It's not far away and has a fantastic view of the water. Maybe we could have a drink there and talk privately?"

A horrible idea. Why invite them to his place unless he was expecting more than a drink? What if he and Danny had found out about her connection to Eduardo? The last thing she needed was an interrogation, or worse.

"Casey, what do you think?" Judging from Kendal's pensive expression, she wasn't sure about this either.

"I'd prefer the pub next door."

Randy rubbed his jaw and looked down. "It'd just be us. Danny's got an engagement after tonight's show." He shoved his hands in his pockets. "The thing is, there's something I need to show you at our place."

Kendal grinned. "I'm sure you do."

"It's not like that." His tone was subdued. "It's an object I found that I need your advice about."

"What kind of object?" Kendal asked.

"It's complicated and will lead to questions I can't get into right now."

Not a good answer, in Casey's view.

Kendal scrutinized him. "Why us, Randy?"

"It's obvious you're both smart and trustworthy. In my world, that's a rare quality."

Casey crossed her arms. Here came the manipulative part. "You must have at least one friend you can trust."

Randy raked his fingers through his hair. "They're

all in my brother's pocket. That's what he does. Takes things from me."

"We need to know what the object is before we commit," Casey replied.

Randy glanced at the door, then stepped closer to Kendal and frowned. "It's a knife with dried blood on the blade. I found it in Danny's safe."

The back entrance opened and Danny filled the threshold. "Randy! You were supposed to be right behind me. What's taking so long? I told you I need the makeup in your locker."

"Be right there."

Spotting them, Danny turned on the smile. "Welcome back, ladies."

"Thanks," Kendal said. "We just need a few more seconds with Randy."

He nodded and went back inside.

"I wanted you to see it for yourselves and tell me what I should do," Randy whispered. "Danny doesn't have any cuts on him, so it's not his blood."

"I don't know." An alarm bell had been ringing in Casey's head the moment Randy mentioned dried blood. "That's serious stuff. Maybe you should call the police."

"That's the complicated part, which I obviously don't have time to explain," Randy murmured. "If it makes things easier, leave your names with the concierge, or let your friends know where you are. Give them my address."

Kendal stood straighter, suddenly all business. "We'll decide by the end of the show. Give me your number and I'll call you."

Randy recited it and his address. "Please come by. You don't need to stay long."

As Randy started to leave, Casey said, "My friend Marie lost her gold-hoop earring here last night. Can I check the bathroom?"

"Of course. I'll take you to RJ, too. He keeps found items in his office."

Casey followed him inside. While Randy escorted Kendal down the hall, Casey entered the bathroom. She searched around the sink but found nothing. The small wicker wastebasket was half filled with crumpled paper towels. Covering her hand with a clean towel, she moved the discarded ones around. She lifted the basket and spotted the earring on the grimy linoleum. Lucky Marie.

Casey washed the earring and headed toward RJ's office until she heard Danny's voice coming from the dressing room across the hall.

"Meeting's right after the show," he said. "See you there."

Casey faltered. Had Randy lied about being alone tonight or was Danny talking about something else?

"Randy! Where the hell are you?" He stepped into the hallway and stopped, his eyes widening. "What are you doing in here, pretty lady?"

"Looking for my friend's lost earring. I just found it in the washroom." Casey opened her palm as Randy and Kendal stepped out of RJ's office.

"RJ didn't have it," Randy said.

"He wouldn't." Casey held out her hand. "It was in the bathroom."

"Excellent." Ignoring his brother, Randy entered the dressing room.

"Enjoy the show," Danny said, following him inside and shutting the door.

Casey didn't repeat what she'd overheard until they were back in Kendal's car.

"I hate the condo idea, Kendal."

"I understand, but my gut tells me that Randy's worry about his brother is genuine. So, why not take his suggestion and arrange for backup? Your buddy Denver works nights, doesn't he?"

"He rotates, and I have no idea if he's patrolling this zone."

"It wouldn't hurt to find out. Meanwhile, we have time to kill, so why not see the show?"

"I can't sit through another night of hysterical women and blaring music. Besides, we need to discuss potential scenarios and come up with a strategy."

"Can we at least watch Randy tear his jeans off?" Kendal asked. "I know you like that part."

"You like it better than me."

Kendal chuckled. "True."

# ELEVEN

Gyrating Handy Randy dropped his tool belt on the floor and flashed a megawatt smile. His routine seemed silly and overdone to Casey this time, but the audience loved it. So did Kendal.

"I could keep him busy while you look through the condo for anything incriminating," Kendal said, fanning her flushed face with a Man Cave brochure.

Casey snorted. "Thanks for the offer, but not necessary."

She and Kendal had debated about whether to go to Randy's condo. Casey had also called Lou to let him know what was happening. She wasn't surprised when he insisted on coming along.

"What about Summer?" she asked. "We don't know how long we'll be or how this'll play out."

"I'll see if she can stay over at a friend's or with my mom and get back to ya."

Lou called again less than ten minutes later, saying Summer had arranged to stay with her BFF, Stacy. He added, "You don't have to do this, you know."

"I know, but if Randy's telling the truth and the knife's a murder weapon, I'll call the cops right away.

This whole thing could be wrapped up tonight."

"You make it sound easy, but I'm still worried."

"How about I try to talk Randy into meeting us in his lobby? He said a concierge's on duty."

"Sounds a bit better."

The problem with bringing Lou was that Randy might not want to talk in front of him. Lou finally agreed to stay out of sight until she signaled otherwise. Now, as Casey watched the men take their final bows, she was second-guessing the whole plan.

"Kendal, I've changed my mind about going to the condo."

"What? No."

"It's just too risky."

Kendal disagreed because she was enjoying this mission. What if Randy was setting them up, though? What if he pulled a weapon on them? All questions she'd raised earlier which Kendal dismissed as highly unlikely, given that Randy had invited them to let the world know where they were.

On the way to Kendal's car, Casey said, "Even after telling you what I overheard Danny say, why do you still want to go there?"

"That conversation might have had nothing to do with Randy. He could be meeting with Alden to plot Eduardo's death." Kendal looked at her. "Could you live with yourself if he died because you chickened out on a chance to stop Danny? What if the guy decides that Lily's a loose end who can identify him, and he goes after her tonight?"

Casey frowned. "You're making me feel guilty."

"For good reason. Lives are at stake."

"Including ours, if things go south." Casey turned to see if any of the performers were emerging from the back entrance. "We should ask Randy to bring what he wants to show us to the lobby or outside the building."

"If it's a murder weapon, do you honestly think he'll display it in a common area?" Kendal replied. "Come on, Casey. My gut tells me he won't hurt us, and you know my intuition's damn near perfect, right? Besides, Lou'll be there."

"Damn near is not the same as a hundred percent, and I'm not okay with putting my husband in danger."

"Look, I came with you tonight as a favor 'cause you're my friend and I love you. Even searched a dirty alley for the earring of someone I can't stand. And remember, we're doing this to keep Lily from being dragged into a murder trial, so try to relax. I've got this. We probably won't need to stay more than a few minutes."

The extra layer of guilt was working. She did owe Kendal. Casey got in the car and peered out of the windshield.

"If it'll make you feel better, let Denver Davies know what's going on," Kendal added.

Denver wouldn't be happy, but perhaps he could persuade Kendal not to go inside the condo. She called him. Turned out Denver was on duty tonight and still patrolling in this zone.

After Casey brought him up to speed, Denver said, "Going inside that condo isn't smart, Casey. If the object really is a murder weapon, you shouldn't even be in the same room with it."

"I know, but Kendal disagrees. Maybe you can get through to her. I'm putting you on speaker."

Casey held the phone between her and Kendal and listened to Denver's lecture. As she expected, all Kendal did was grunt and make faces at Casey.

"It's not illegal to accept an invitation to the guy's home, right?" Kendal asked him. "He's not a suspect in any crime?"

"Not that I'm aware of, but you must realize how sketchy this sounds."

"Denver, in my job I deal with sketchy nearly every day," Kendal retorted. "If Randy has evidence that could solve at least one crime, then it's worth the trip. So, why don't you drop by and have a look yourself."

Judging from his loud huff, Denver wasn't pleased.

"Casey, have you talked to Bojaski?" he asked.

"Yeah, I called him before I met up with Kendal, but he didn't seem interested in what I had to say."

"I'll call him."

"Can I text you with updates?" Casey asked.

"Yeah, but depending on what's going on, there's no guarantee I'll see it right away."

"Understood. I'll let you know when we're there." She ended the call and saw Kendal looking up directions to Randy's condo.

"He lives only a six-minute drive from here." Kendal turned to her. "Have we decided what approach to take? Subtle and flirty or direct and businesslike?"

"If we're really doing this, then friendly but direct."

"Fine. I'll do most of the talking. You don't have to say a word if you don't want to."

Casey doubted it would play out that way. "So, we

won't eat or drink anything that Randy might offer, okay? He could spike something."

"If you say so."

"At the first sign of trouble, I'm calling 9-1-1."

"I wouldn't expect anything less."

Lou texted her. He'd reached the address she sent him. Casey's stomach knotted.

Danny emerged from the building. Carrying a costume, he jumped into his Jaguar. Casey hadn't seen Alden tonight, but Danny could have let him in through the back door during the show.

"Follow him," Casey said. "Let's see if big brother's going to the condo."

"Good idea." She started the engine. "It won't take long to figure out if he's heading there or not."

Danny made a couple of left turns and headed west.

"If he makes a right turn, then he's probably heading home." Kendal stayed three car lengths back from the Jag.

Danny sped toward the Stanley Park causeway that would take him onto the Lions Gate Bridge and into West Vancouver.

When he made no right turn, Casey's shoulders relaxed. "Looks like he won't be joining us."

"Unless he's on a quick errand."

They reached Randy's complex and saw Lou waiting out front.

"You know," Casey remarked, "it's not too late to back out, Kendal."

"It'll be fine, trust me."

Casey stared at her. "Every time you said that in

school, we wound up in hot water."

"I've learned a lot since then."

"Like how to be more devious?"

Kendal smiled. "It's a gift."

# TWELVE

As Casey had feared, Randy refused to bring the knife to the lobby in his building. Kendal tried her best to persuade him, but no luck. So, here they were in his condo. Immense floor-to-ceiling windows overlooking Vancouver's Coal Harbour and Stanley Park were the most breathtaking aspect of this pricey place. The black-and-white décor was bland and the collage of selfies was a testament to mammoth-sized egos. Silver-framed photos of Danny, either on stage or posing by European landmarks, littered tabletops. For every four shots of Danny, there was one of Randy. Only two photos showed them together in what appeared to be a stage play.

"Would either of you like a glass of wine?" Randy asked.

"Sure," Kendal answered.

Casey frowned. What had happened to their don't-drink-or-eat strategy? "Not for me, thanks."

Although Lou was right outside Randy's door and Denver was patrolling this zone tonight, she still felt vulnerable.

Randy removed a key from his pocket and headed

for a brightly lit wine cabinet with mullioned glass doors. "Red, white, or rosé?"

"Red, please." Kendal ambled closer to the collection. "If you two live alone, why keep the cabinet locked?"

"Danny doesn't want me dipping into his collection. He doesn't know I found the key ages ago." Randy stepped back. "All the reds are on the right. Choose whatever you want."

While Kendal perused the bottles and commented on the excellent selection, Casey's phone pinged. A text from Lou. *R U OK?*

Casey responded with a thumbs-up emoji.

"Let's go with this Beaujolais," Kendal suggested.

Randy replaced the bottle with one from the corner of the bottom row. "It'll take him a while to figure it out," he added. "Danny prefers the hard stuff. This collection's to impress guests."

He retrieved a corkscrew and two long-stemmed glasses, then glanced at Casey. "Are you sure you don't want a small glass?"

Given that Kendal had chosen the bottle and they were watching Danny pour, Casey figured the wine was safe. "Maybe half a glass."

He handed her a four-ounce portion, then raised his glass. "To trustworthy friends."

This was the second time he'd mentioned the word trustworthy this evening.

Kendal sipped the wine. "Incredible!"

Casey also tried it. "Wow." A big improvement over the sweet, twelve-dollar special Lou bought last week. She was tempted to sneak into the hallway so he could try it.

Randy led them to a black leather sofa facing the windows and sat in the chair to their left. Kendal slowly crossed her legs. While Randy focused on her rising hemline, Casey tapped the record button on her phone and tucked it into the outer pocket of her purse.

"Did your brother decorate this room?" Kendal asked.

He smiled. "The selfies are a giveaway, huh?"

"Pretty much."

Peering into his wine glass, Randy's smile faded.

"You said you had something to show us?" Casey asked.

"Before I do, can I ask a little more about you?"

Right, here came the game-playing part.

"At first, I thought you were cops, but you're too chill." Elbows on thighs, Randy leaned forward. "So, what's your interest in me, 'cause I don't think it's a threesome." He zeroed in on Kendal. "Please tell me I'm wrong."

Casey knew that the sparkle in her friend's eyes and the glowing cheeks weren't solely about hormones. Kendal loved back-and-forth exchanges to see how much information she could learn from someone without revealing too much about herself.

"You're right, we're not cops, and this isn't about sex," Kendal began. "Casey's a friend of Eduardo's, and she believes he's being framed for the murder of a woman named Daphne Reynard, one of Man Cave's patrons."

Whoa. Too much information? On the other hand,

Randy's reaction could reveal a lot.

"I heard about it." Randy tugged on his shirt collar. "Just awful." He took a gulp of wine. "Who does he think set him up?"

Casey held her breath. This would be tricky. She noted the long gaze Kendal gave Randy before saying, "Someone connected to Man Cave, but he has no idea who."

Randy clasped the wine glass with both hands and shook his head. Interesting that Randy didn't seem surprised by Kendal's answer.

"Why does he think it's connected to us?"

"The police found something of Eduardo's at the crime scene, but he says it was stolen from his locker," Casey replied. "He keeps his locker open during a show, so I'm wondering if you saw anyone take something from it?"

Randy gently swirled the wine for several seconds.

"Danny took Eduardo's gold thong. I thought it was just a dumb prank." He peered at Kendal. "Don't tell me they found it in her house."

"They did," Casey replied. Good guess. Too good?

Randy stood and headed toward the dining area as she exchanged a wary glance with Kendal. He stopped in front of a water-color portrait of the brothers, then turned to them.

"My brother's angry and unstable. He thought Eduardo got too many tips, which was ripping off the rest of us. When he heard that RJ planned to make Eduardo the headliner, he lost it." Randy shook his head. "You've just confirmed my worst nightmare."

"Which is?" Kendal asked.

He took a deep breath. "That Danny killed Mrs. Reynard and framed Eduardo."

Kendal plunked her glass on the coffee table.

Casey's heartbeat quickened as she snuck a peek at her phone to make sure it was still recording.

"Why would he kill her instead of Eduardo?" Kendal asked.

"No idea. All I know is that he's cruel and irrational." Randy swept his hand through his hair. "Last Sunday, Danny came home about one in the morning. I'd just gone to bed but wanted to ask him about a text alert from the bank, so I got up. That's when I saw him put something in the safe. Danny was muttering to himself, obviously in a lousy mood, so I went back to bed."

Randy removed the painting. Behind it was a small safe with a keypad.

"This week, I made a point of searching for the code." He pressed each digit slowly. "Found it this afternoon."

"Do you want us to look away?" Casey asked.

"Don't care. It's his shit, not mine."

She and Kendal stood. Casey couldn't see the numbers from this angle, but Randy was right. It didn't matter. She was more concerned about the safe's contents. If Randy pulled out a handgun, they were in deep trouble. Clutching her phone, Casey backed away, ready to call 9-1-1.

Randy removed an object wrapped in a white towel. "This is what I wanted to show you."

He unfolded the towel and revealed a dagger with a

handle shaped like the head of a snake. Dried blood covered the blade and stained the towel. He placed the towel and dagger on the dining table.

"Holy shit," Kendal murmured.

Casey's phone pinged again, and she flinched.

Randy looked up, his jaw tightening. "Something wrong?"

She glanced at Lou's text. "Just my husband, wondering how long I'll be. He's close by." Without giving Randy a chance to respond, she said, "If this is a murder weapon, why wouldn't Danny have got rid of it?"

"Because it's his idea of leverage to keep me in line," Randy mumbled. "If I do something to piss him off, he'll tell the cops that I killed Mrs. Reynard, if that's her blood."

"Would your fingerprints be on that knife?" Kendal asked.

"No, but I doubt his are either, so it'd make both of us suspects. I wouldn't put it past him to plant other evidence against me. My brother's always enjoyed making my life miserable." Randy's face flushed red as he glared at the weapon. "What I need your advice on, is how to turn Danny in without him finding out it was me."

Raising one eyebrow, Kendal said, "You'd really do that to your brother?"

"I have to. Danny's spinning out of control with the coke addiction." Randy met her gaze. "I'm afraid the rage'll get so bad that he'll kill me too."

Casey again glanced at Kendal. Things had become too intense. Time to call Denver.

"There's tons of drugs in his room," Randy added.

"If we made it look like someone burgled this place, then called the cops, they'd arrest him."

*We?* Casey stared at the guy. Randy didn't need their help staging a burglary, but involving them gave him coconspirators. He wouldn't have to take all the blame if the cops decided that Randy wasn't an innocent bystander. Did the guy think she and Kendal were that dumb?

"It won't work," Kendal said. "I spotted closed-circuit cameras in your lobby, so our arrival's on record, and the concierge knows we're here to see you."

"Why not leave an anonymous tip through Crime Stoppers?" Casey asked.

Randy shrugged. "Who knows how fast their response would be and that knife's been here nearly a week. Knowing Danny, he's getting antsy to move it. Maybe even tonight."

Casey's stomach clenched at the thought of Danny showing up while they were still here. With Lou in the hallway, things could get nasty in no time.

"I have a friend who'll know what to do," she said. "Denver's had a lot of experience dealing with tricky situations."

Randy rubbed his temple. "I dunno about involving more people."

"It'll be okay," Kendal said. "We trust Denver. He's a calm, levelheaded guy."

Before Randy could say no, Casey hurried out of the condo and found Lou pacing the hallway.

He hurried up to her. "Everything okay?" he whispered. "What's happening?"

"Randy showed us what he says is the dagger that killed Daphne Reynard. Apparently, he saw Danny put it in the wall safe."

"Do you believe him?"

"Doesn't matter. I'm calling Denver." She tapped his number, grateful that he answered right away.

"We're on our way and I'll call Bojaski," Denver said after she described the situation. "You've stepped into a big pile of doo-doo this time, Casey."

"Blame the man with the gold satin thong." She hung up and turned to Lou. "If you see a big, muscular guy with dark hair heading this way, text me."

"The brother?"

"Yeah, and watch out for a tall skinny guy, too. He's the drug dealer."

Casey re-entered the condo and stayed by the door. She didn't want Randy changing his mind and taking off. She also worried that Danny would return any moment.

"What did your friend say?" Randy asked her. "Will he help?"

"Yeah, he'll be here soon."

"Excellent." Kendal smiled. "Now, let's enjoy this scrumptious wine."

Randy plunked back into the chair and took a gulp. Kendal waved Casey over, but she preferred to stay by the door. Randy drank and rambled on about Danny's long history of bullying and petty crimes.

"Has Danny ever been arrested?" Kendal asked.

"There've been close calls, but he's always talked his way out of trouble, with my help." Randy gazed at the view of the harbor, his expression glum. "He's made me cover for him more than once and I'm so done with that."

Kendal asked Randy questions about himself, but his answers were short and vague.

Casey's phone pinged. Another text from Lou. *Cops R here.* Relief swept through her as the doorbell rang. "My friend's arrived."

She opened the door to uniformed officers accompanied by a hefty, forty-something man identifying himself as Detective Constable Bojaski.

Randy's eyes bugged out as he turned to Casey.

"You said you were calling a friend."

"My friend's a cop with the Vancouver Police Department."

Randy staggered backward. "I'm dead."

# THIRTEEN

"I'm glad Eduardo's truly free," Lily said as she drove the bus through the late afternoon traffic.

"Thanks to you." Standing beside her, Casey added, "After you identified Danny as the guy who claimed to be Marcos, I gave his picture to the cops. Sure enough, the fraud victims confirmed that Danny was the man calling himself Eduardo. If you hadn't given me the bracelet, they wouldn't have found Danny's prints on the box it came in."

"They would have caught him at some point. The man's not that bright."

"True. Even with Lou in the hallway and the door to his condo open, Danny just walked right in and found himself facing a bunch of cops with guns drawn. The guy seemed clueless, but maybe he was high, I don't know."

While the cops were arresting Danny for murder and possession of a large quantity of cocaine, his confusion erupted into a terrifying rage. Thankfully, she and Kendal were being ushered out of the condo when he lunged at Randy. She could still picture the spittle dripping from Danny's mouth while he ranted about his brother planting the drugs. He insisted that Randy had masterminded Daphne Reynard's murder. The last she saw of Randy, he was answering Bojaski's questions. Neither she nor Kendal had heard from him since, nor did she expect to.

"Danny's gonna pull me into this, isn't he?" Lily asked. "He'll say I was with him at the time of the murder."

"Maybe, but testifying is months away. By then you'll be divorced and Frank will be long out of the picture. If he doesn't watch the news, he won't even hear about the trial."

"He's never cared about what's going on outside his own little world." She glanced at Casey. "Will MPT give me a hard time?"

"Stan made it clear to Gwyn and your supervisors that you were instrumental in solving two major crimes primarily because of your engagement with riders."

"Nice spin." Lily slowed the bus. "I see Eduardo at the next stop."

"I'll find us a seat."

She found an empty spot midway down. Eduardo could have picked a better place to meet, but he insisted the bus was safer for him. When she asked why he was concerned about safety, Eduardo said he'd explain when they met. He sounded worried, though.

Lily eased up to the stop and opened the door.

Oh geez, not Eduardo's sexiest getup. His neon yellow polo shirt and green pants with a yellow-and-black-diamond pattern drew smiles and a chuckle or two from passengers. He carried what was shaped like a painting wrapped in brown paper.

Eduardo greeted Lily, then sauntered down the aisle. "Hola, Miss Casey. Thank you for meeting with me."

Here in public, the heavy accent didn't surprise her. She looked him up and down. "What have you been up to today?"

"A golf date with lady friend who loves the sport. I also painted something for you." Eduardo handed her his gift. "In deepest gratitude for all your help."

Oh, no. She envisioned a naked self-portrait of Eduardo on black velvet. "You shouldn't have gone to so much trouble."

"Is great pleasure, Miss Casey," he said. "Because of you, RJ has made me the headlining act."

Two teenage girls sat behind them while a senior wearing a wide-brimmed hat, sunglasses, and baggy clothes, took the seat across from them and one back.

"Congratulations on your promotion," Casey said. "So, what did you want to talk to me about?"

Eduardo's pleased expression vanished. "Yesterday, a motorcycle tried to run me down."

Casey lowered her voice. "You're kidding. Did you get a look at the driver?"

"His visor was dark, but I think I know who it is. I need your help one more time to prove I am right."

"Why would someone want to hurt you? You weren't involved in Danny's arrest and he's still in jail. My cop friend told me that Alden was picked up on drug trafficking charges in Alberta, so he's not around either."

"Ah! Then I definitely know who the motorcyclist is." Gold-flecked eyes blinked at her. "On my first night of work with Man Cave, Randy rode a motorbike to work. I also think Danny is not smart enough to run a credit card fraud scam."

"Alden could be," Casey replied. "For all we know, he was stealing cards from women too."

"Is possible, I guess. But I remembered something yesterday," Eduardo said. "Danny asked Randy if he'd sent money to Cayman Bank. They would not need international banking for our paychecks."

Casey looked out the window, her thoughts swirling. Was Danny's accusation about his brother correct? What if Randy was the one who killed Daphne Reynard? If so, then Randy had planted the weapon in the safe for her and Kendal's benefit. The creep could have used them to help persuade the cops that Danny was guilty of multiple crimes.

"None of the other performers ride motorcycles, Miss Casey," Eduardo added. "I asked them all, and Brian agreed this is true."

"Son of a bitch." Casey huffed. "Showing us that bloodstained dagger was a smooth move."

"Dagger?" Eduardo blinked at her. "Did it have the head of a snake?"

Casey's shoulders tightened. "You've seen it?"

"Si. On first night of performing." Eduardo's tone became hushed. "Randy bought it for Danny, who pretended to slash everyone. I thought he was loco."

Lily slowed for the next stop. A guy in his late teens came up from the back and tripped over the foot of the senior across the aisle.

"Asshole," the teen muttered, regaining his balance.

Casey stared at the kid while the senior slid his foot back. The senior kept his head lowered.

"Danny put the knife in his locker before going on stage," Eduardo continued. "Randy told me it is common and cheap, like his brother, but I saw the same dagger in Randy's locker."

The back of Case's neck tingled. "There were two of them?"

"Si." His expression became animated. "Randy switched them when Danny was on stage. I did not think anything about it then. But now? I think he planned something bad against Danny for long time." Eduardo's exuberance faded. "I did not notice, but Randy must have worn gloves when he switched daggers. He always uses latex gloves to put on the body oil."

Casey nodded. "So, he kept the dagger with Danny's prints on it and waited for an opportunity, which started to percolate when he met you. It came together once he realized you and Daphne Reynard had a relationship." She sat up straighter. "Danny's disastrous dinner date with Daphne would've prompted Randy to act fast. If Daphne learned about the credit card ring on the news, the brothers would worry she'd call the cops on them."

"But why frame me?" Eduardo asked.

Casey absently tapped her finger against her cheek while she thought about it. "Two reasons. One is that Danny wanted you gone so he could be the headliner. Second, Randy framed you to make Danny believe that Randy had his back. Obviously, Danny knew that Randy killed Daphne. He was in on the scheme or he wouldn't have taken Lily's phone to send you that text. But Randy's smart enough to know the charge against you wouldn't stick, especially since you weren't the only man at Daphne's house the night of the murder."

"And Danny is not so smart," Eduardo muttered.

"Not enough to realize he was about to become the second and more convincing scapegoat. Maybe he was too arrogant to think Randy would betray him like that."

"Now Danny is out of his way and I am next," Eduardo mumbled. "Randy is worried I saw him switch daggers."

Casey turned to him. "Did he see you?"

"I walked in the room while he was doing it," Eduardo replied. "He did not turn his head. Still, maybe he knew."

"Peripheral vision," Casey murmured. "I think you're right about Randy wanting to hurt you. We need to call the police."

While Lily eased the bus to the next stop, passengers made their way up the aisle. Casey glanced at the senior's long leg, again stretched out and in the way. She noticed the tanned ankle beneath his sweatpants and the expensive running shoe. An uneasy feeling took hold, and then she recalled a photo in the brothers' condo. One of Randy on stage in makeup that made him appear decades older. The senior took off his sunglasses. Casey gasped at the familiar blue eyes glaring at her. Oh, crap.

She started to call 9-1-1 as Randy grabbed one of three tween girls walking past him. He jumped up and held the snakehead dagger to her throat. The girl screamed and struggled, but she was no match for him.

"Drop the phone or I'll kill her!"

Her companions ran toward the front exit. Lily had already opened the doors.

Casey did as he asked. "Just relax. No one needs to get hurt."

A few frightened passengers scrambled off the bus. Others seemed frozen in place. Lily glanced over her shoulder and gave a slight nod, signaling that she'd pressed the panic alarm. MPT dispatchers would hear everything and call for help.

"Randy! You cannot do this!" Eduardo stood up.

"Shut up, asshole."

"Let the girl go, Randy, and leave before the police arrive." Casey's heart slammed against her chest. "The driver's pressed the alarm and our dispatchers can hear you."

"Screw that. I'm hanging onto this bargaining chip." He shook the girl, who was clutching his massive forearm with both hands. "I should have tried again with the motorcycle, Eduardo. My mistake."

Casey glanced at Lily, hoping she'd left for safety. Instead, Lily removed the hairspray from her pocket. Damn. If she tried to use it as a weapon, things could get a whole lot worse.

"Lily!" Eduardo raced toward her. "Stay away!"

Randy yelled, "Get back here, loser!"

Eduardo hauled Lily off the bus while Randy struggled to contain the sobbing, squirming girl.

"Stay still!" He shook her until the poor girl's legs

buckled.

"I'll take her place," Casey said. "Let her go."

"No." Randy hauled the girl to her feet.

Casey swallowed, her throat dry. "Tell me what you want."

"Freedom." Sweat poured down his face. "I wasn't lying about Danny's bullying or the violence and coke addiction. I needed to take control of things before my psycho brother killed me. But Eduardo saw and heard things he shouldn't."

"You two work at the same place." Casey frowned. "So, why here?"

"His death couldn't be connected to anyone from Man Cave, and an old guy on a bus has a better shot at disappearing in the crowd."

Not anymore. Distant sirens grew louder. The fury on Randy's face turned to wariness, then fear. Why wasn't he leaving?

Eduardo crept back on board behind Randy, carrying the hairspray. For crying out loud, what did he think he was doing? Casey held her breath and forced herself not to look at him.

"The cops are almost here." She returned Randy's stare. "Last chance to escape."

Eduardo edged right up to him and yelled, "Randy!"

As Randy looked back, Eduardo sprayed his eyes. Randy yelped and bent over, releasing the girl and dropping the knife. Swearing, he covered his face with both hands and collapsed onto a seat. The girl raced off the bus while patrol cars screeched to a halt.

"Eduardo, go outside," Casey said. "The cops are

here."

"I will not leave until you are safe."

"I *am* safe."

The police charged through both entrances and ordered Eduardo to drop the hairspray. Casey swiftly explained what was going on.

"Oh my, that is long blade." Swaying slightly, Eduardo wiped his perspiring brow. "You are so brave, Miss Casey."

"You, too." She glanced at the armpit stains darkening his shirt.

By the time officers had interviewed her and Lily and taken Randy away, Casey was anxious to go home. The cops wouldn't be releasing the bus for a while, so Stan volunteered to give her and Lily a lift back to MPT. Casey was waiting for him on the sidewalk when Eduardo approached, carrying the painting.

"They've finished interviewing you?" Casey asked.

"Si." He presented the painting. "You forgot this."

"Right." She had indeed forgotten.

"It is I who should be giving thanks. Without you, I would still be in jail or dead." He shuddered. "I must depart to prepare for tonight's date. I am escorting a lady to Theater Under the Stars."

"Have fun." Shifting the painting, she noticed that some of the brown paper was torn near the top.

"Maybe you will come to our show before we leave town?"

"We'll see." She didn't have the heart to say that the idea held no appeal.

"Adiós, Miss Casey." He leaned forward and whispered in her ear, without the accent. "You're a hell of a woman, and I'll always be grateful."

"Thanks." She grinned. "And you're welcome."

While Eduardo strutted away, Casey studied the torn bit of paper. Dare she look at her gift in public? The decision wasn't hard.

Peeking through the torn paper, she was stunned by the vibrant hues of green, yellow, and brown. Casey widened the tear and gaped at delicate brushstrokes of sunlight glowing through the branches of a cedar forest. The painting radiated mystery, beauty, and serenity. As she pored over the piece, Eduardo's words echoed in her head . . . Light from darkness and the hope of great possibilities, from a true artista and freer of truth.

# BOOKS BY DEBRA PURDY KONG

## Casey Holland Mysteries

The Opposite of Dark (2011)
Deadly Accusations (2012)
Beneath the Bleak New Moon (2013)
The Deep End (2014)
Knock Knock (2017)
The Blade Man (2020)

# ABOUT THE AUTHOR

Debra Purdy Kong's volunteer experiences, criminology diploma, and various jobs inspired her to write mysteries set in BC's Lower Mainland. Her employment as a campus security patrol and communications officer provided the background for her Casey Holland transit security novels.

Debra has published short stories in a variety of genres as well as personal essays, and articles for publications such as *Chicken Soup for the Bride's Soul, B.C. Parent Magazine,* and *The Vancouver Sun.* She is a facilitator for the Creative Writing Program through Port Moody Recreation and a long-time member of Crime Writers of Canada. She lives in British Columbia, Canada.

For more information about Debra and her books, visit her website at www.debrapurdykong.com
or contact her at dpurdykong@gmail.com